AT LAST

BOOK ELEVEN ~ WALKER FAMILY SERIES

BERNADETTE MARIE

5 PRINCE PUBLISHING

Published by 5 PRINCE PUBLISHING & BOOKS, LLC

PO Box 865, Arvada, CO 80001

www.5PrinceBooks.com

ISBN digital: 978-1-63112-246-0

ISBN print: 978-1-63112-247-7

Cover Credit: B. Soehner

To Stan,
From friends to forever.
I love you!

ACKNOWLEDGMENTS

For T, N, G, S, J, Mom, and Sissy – I simply couldn't ask for better people to be in my life. I am so blessed.

For Cate – I am grateful to you every day. Thank you for making sense of my crazy nonsense.

For my readers – Thank you for loving Lydia and Phillip and wanting their stories. This was an amazing book to have the privilege to write.

For my Book Hive – Thank you for being on the front lines for me. Your loyalty is priceless.

For my tribe – Thank you for the honor of your friendship and your knowledge.

AT LAST

BOOK ELEVEN ~ THE WALKER FAMILY SERIES

Bernadette Marie

CHAPTER 1

*I*t had been hard enough to stand in that very spot and watch everything she and her friends had built burn to the ground, but nearly two months after the fire, Lydia Morgan thought it was even more heartbreaking to watch progress— which meant the remains of the existing structure had to come all the way down.

Ella Walker, her lawyer, had been key in making sure that the insurance company was working on Lydia's behalf, and that of the others who lost their business that early morning in May.

She'd been on site every day since the fire. It certainly hadn't been the way she'd wanted to reintegrate herself into the community after having been gone for nearly a year, but it wasn't something she could control. And part of her therapy was learning how to let go of control and adjust.

Lydia owned most of the town, both the buildings and the businesses. She had taken after her mother in that sense, together their names were on quite a bit of real estate.

The *Bridal Mecca* had been a special project she had taken on with Pearl Walker. It had been a big deal for a Morgan and a

1

Walker to go into business together. The families had feuded for years. It had not only been one of the most profitable partnerships Lydia had ever entered into, but it also grew her family, literally. Pearl had fallen in love with Lydia's brother Tyson, who was also one of the owners of the building.

Now, that building and business was nothing but a pile of rubble, but it would absolutely be rebuilt.

Lydia walked back to her car, pulling off the hard hat she kept in the back seat. She ran her fingers through her short crop of hair, which Audrey had cut just the day before. Lydia always wore her hair short, but while she'd been gone, she'd given up that control too, and had let it grow. After two months, it had been time to take back that part of her identity.

Just as she opened the door to her car, the familiar personal truck of Phillip Smythe pulled into the lot.

A year ago, she would have climbed into her car and driven over the curb to escape talking to him. But that was then. Her therapy had carried her through that as well—her misguided relationship with the man.

Phillip stepped out of his truck. His police uniform had been replaced with a pair of jeans and a pearl-snapped shirt. The buckle on his belt was a souvenir of the days he'd team roped and won. His boots were worn, and the bill of his ball cap shielded his eyes.

His long legs carried him toward her, slowly, as if he were still afraid to talk to her.

She wasn't sure if his apprehension was because he was never sure if she'd bite his head off, or if he was still spooked by what had happened to her a year ago.

Again, part of her therapy covered her feelings for Phillip Smythe, and she had plenty of them.

"Looks like they're making progress," he said, lifting the bill of his cap to reveal those gray eyes she remembered from long ago.

"I suppose. It's hard to think progress means taking down what was there."

Phillip tucked his hands into the front pockets of his jeans and rocked back on his heels. "Your hair looks good."

"Thanks. I needed to return to some normality. I have no idea how other women wear their hair long."

"Short has always suited you," he complimented, and she watched as he ground his heel into the dirt. "Are you headed out?"

"I have a meeting this afternoon with a new bride looking for a venue."

"And you have a few to choose from."

She smiled wide. "You know, my goal is to own the entire town."

"You're well on your way."

"I'll see you around," she said as she pulled open the door to her car and climbed in.

Phillip walked toward the fence that had been put up around the shell of the *Bridal Mecca* and Lydia sat in her car and let out a long breath. It had been nearly fifteen years since she'd had a civil conversation with the man, and she'd allowed herself to be comforted by his arm around her the night that the *Bridal Mecca* burnt down. She figured he'd come around more often after that. He'd been everywhere she'd turned for years, but over the past two months his presence had been scarce.

It was as foreign to have him stay away from her as it was for her to want him around—at least a little bit.

After she'd been kidnapped, sexually assaulted, and left for dead, she realized holding a grudge against Phillip was a waste of her time and energy. Any anger and resentment she had toward him had always been her fault.

The therapy she'd gone through had taught her how to approach their past, and to accept that he was a daily part of her life.

She supposed if she wanted to spend time with him, and truly see if her therapy had worked, she would need to lead the conversation.

Opening her door, Lydia stepped out and stood in front of her car. "Hey, Smythe," she yelled to be heard over the construction noise.

He turned to look at her, and then walked toward her.

"You're not on duty, huh?"

Phillip shook his head. "No."

"Well then you have some time."

"Time for what?"

"Why don't you have lunch with me? I'd love some company, and I want to try that new Greek place on the edge of town."

"I thought you had a meeting."

"Later," she confirmed.

Phillip thoughtfully bit down on his lip. "I could go for some lunch. I can just meet you over there."

She'd have offered to drive, but maybe meeting him would be best. What if she found being in his presence for more than a few minutes at a time made her hate him again? What if seeing her broken had pushed him away for good?

"I'll meet you there," she agreed and watched as he walked to his truck.

She knew he'd never drive away until she had, so she pulled out of the parking lot and started driving toward the restaurant. Phillip followed her in his truck, and when she'd looked back in her mirror her stomach tightened.

It had been a long year of healing. She couldn't go back on her fifteen years of resentment and just assume he'd accept that she wanted to be friends. There were also secrets she still kept, and things would certainly change between them if he found out.

Lydia gripped her steering wheel tighter. This was lunch. Lunch with a man she'd pushed away for years. She had learned she had to take things one moment at a time. This was just one moment in the rest of her life.

Lunch.

She could handle lunch.

CHAPTER 2

*P*hillip rubbed his palms on his thighs as they stopped
at a traffic light. He'd been to the Greek restaurant,
but the invitation to dine with Lydia intrigued him, and scared
him to death.

She'd stopped talking to him nearly fifteen years ago, packed
up, and moved away. A year or so later, she turned back up in
town and started buying up businesses and making a name for
herself.

Even though she wouldn't have anything to do with him, he'd
made sure he was present in her life since then. But she'd always
made it clear he wasn't welcome. Still, old feelings ran deep, and
it was hard to stay away.

He'd worried over her since the minute he'd helped her out of
that house, bloodied and beaten a year ago. She'd left after that,
opting to take time to heal. For a while she was at a hospital, but
no one knew where. Then she and her mother moved to Hawaii
for a bit. Lydia's mother had returned before Lydia was ready to
come home.

The day he'd driven by her house and had seen her in the

window, he'd thought he might have a heart attack. She was finally home, where she belonged. Both times Lydia had gone away had broken his heart and his spirit. The fact that she was willing to talk to him at all should make him feel whole, but it didn't yet.

He'd been scarce for the past few months just to give her time to settle in. It wasn't as if he hadn't been busy in his own life. The police department never had a down time.

They'd caught the last of the men who had been burglarizing the businesses in town and setting small fires. The fire at the *Bridal Mecca* hadn't been set intentionally, but happened when the man had broken into Jessie Hanson's photography studio and was carrying out her computer. He'd tripped on a cord and had knocked over one of her lights. That had been what caused the spark that started the fire.

When he'd met with Lydia and the rest of the women from the *Bridal Mecca,* to give them the news, Lydia hadn't made up a reason that she had to go, or that he should go. He'd been invited to sit with them all, at Pearl's Bridal Boutique, and have coffee. There had been a few times he'd even caught Lydia watching him, and when he looked at her, she would smile.

She'd done that once, a long time ago, but he'd gotten used to the scowls and muttered unkind words over the years. How odd was it that he didn't know, now, what to make of gracious Lydia?

Phillip pulled into the lot behind Lydia, and they each parked. He watched as she climbed from her car, more aware of her surroundings than he'd remembered her being. She locked the door and stood by the entrance to wait for him.

Phillip climbed out of his truck and slowly crossed the lot toward her.

"I didn't know you liked Greek food," he said.

She smiled, and still he wasn't sure what to do with that.

"I found that I quite enjoy gyros. Their reviews are stellar when it comes to their gyro platter. It's big enough for two. We could share it."

Her voice was soft and kind, and it stirred up old emotions that squeezed his chest.

"I could go for that." He reached for the door and pulled it open. Lydia walked through and immediately talked to the hostess that sat them in a booth by the window.

He wasn't sure he'd be good company seated there. There was a tendency, as an officer of the law, to watch the many actions and reactions of people who walked in and out of the shops that surrounded them. He could easily be more attentive to his environment than to the company he kept, even when he was off duty.

But he'd focus on the woman seated across from him.

Lydia seemed smaller to him. She stood no taller than five foot three, and he knew from having bought her many things, years ago, even after weeks on an ice cream binge she never was bigger than a size nine. Those charcoal eyes held command over any conversation, and he'd seen huge men give in to what she wanted just by the tone of her voice.

The woman seated across from him now had a softness to her. Her shoulders hunched in slightly, taking off the rough exterior. Though she'd cut her hair short again, it too seemed to have a softness to it.

"How are all the businesses?" he asked after they had ordered their meal, and he noted that she'd ordered a decaf coffee. That was something new too. Lydia ran on caffeine.

"They're all doing well. I met with all the girls from the *Bridal Mecca* the other day, and they're all doing better than they were in the building. But they all think that's because we got a lot of publicity for opening shop so quickly in different locations. Audrey even took in the stylists from that other salon that had been set fire to. Their insurance company is dragging their feet."

"I'm glad it's going well. I was in Audrey's shop the other day. Nichole cut my hair."

The waitress delivered their drinks, and Phillip instinctively pushed the sugar packets toward her.

"I'm fine with it black. Thank you," she said again with that smile.

"Decaf and no sugar."

Lydia wrapped her hands around the mug. "I did a lot of detoxing, if you will. I let go of a lot of hate and resentment. I started doing yoga instead of running. No more caffeine, and no more sugar."

It was then he noticed the glow that emanated from her skin, and he could see that she was healthy-looking. Maybe he should think about decaf and losing the sugar, himself.

"You look great," he said, and he heard the quiver in his voice.

Lydia lifted her mug to her lips and sipped. "Thank you. I feel great."

How far could this conversation go in public? He wanted to know exactly how she was. How did she overcome everything that bastard had put her through? He'd seen women who had been kidnapped, beaten, and sexually assaulted. Very few of them had clear eyes like Lydia had.

Those clear eyes grew wide when the server delivered the platter and sat it between them on the table.

"Now that's what I was talking about. I'm so happy this place opened up," she cheered as she put her napkin in her lap. "Maybe this would be easier if we sat next to each other."

Phillip had lifted his water to his lips to sip, but was glad he hadn't, because when she said that, he choked on the air he was breathing.

Lydia moved from her side of the table to his as he scooted toward the window. Other than the night of the fire, when he kept his arm around her, this was the closest they'd been in fifteen years.

Phillip watched as she began to assemble her gyro. Steadily, he drew in a breath and let it out again. *Don't get ahead of yourself, cowboy. In another week, she'll hate the sight of you again.* But for that moment he was going to cherish the fact that she wanted to sit next to him, talk to him, and share a meal. It was all he could ask for.

CHAPTER 3

*L*ydia was dying to go for a walk down the lush trails that followed the river through town. However, that was something she couldn't, and wouldn't do alone.

In Hawaii, the condo she'd rented faced the ocean. The path from her place to the beach was only a few hundred feet, but when her mother had left, she'd never gone back down to the beach by herself.

She was fine in her home, back in Georgia. Sure, she'd been abducted from it, but still, she'd let her guard down when that had happened. That guard would never be down again.

She had a security alarm, locks on all her windows and doors, and floodlights on the outside of her house. Before she went to bed each night, she put a chair under the knob on the door, left lights on in the house, and locked her bedroom door. All of it was perfectly normal.

There had been some consideration of getting a dog, but did she really want the pressure of having to take care of it? Not that it would be a big deal, and she worked for herself, so the dog could go with her.

She'd still consider it.

Now she wanted to go for a walk, but she'd want company.

Lydia texted her brother, who had made it a point to be by her side if she needed it. She knew he was working out at the Morgan Ranch, but she texted anyway.

I want to go for a walk. She texted and waited for his reply by loading all of the dishes in the cupboard into the dishwasher. Three times she'd already washed every dish, cup, and fork in her kitchen. But it gave her some peace.

Lydia turned when her phone buzzed on the counter. *Then go for a walk.*

I don't want to be alone. She replied and set the phone back on the counter.

She didn't receive another text.

Once she'd loaded the dishes into the dishwasher, she pulled the sheets off the bed and put them in the washing machine. They'd been freshly laundered the day before, but she wanted them clean again.

After that, she reached for her bottle of Pledge and a rag, then took in after the baseboards and windowsills.

When there was a knock at the door she stood for a moment. Quietly she set the rag and cleaner on the table and reached for her phone. She pulled up the app attached to her doorbell and saw that Pearl was standing on her front step—hair pulled back, exercise clothes on.

"Bastard," she said under her breath, referring to her brother.

Lydia hit the code into the alarm panel to disable it. Then she moved the chair, unbolted the lock, released the lock on the knob, and opened the door to the locked security screen door. She released the deadbolt, and the lock on the handle before opening the door to Pearl.

"Fort Knox, huh?" Pearl asked with a smile.

Lydia tried to remember that Pearl stood there, in the middle of one of her busiest work days, in her walking clothes, because her brother cared enough to send his wife.

"Tyson called you?"

There was no mistaking that was the case as Pearl's cheeks pinked. "He said you wanted to go for a walk. I'm here. I could certainly use a walk, and Sunshine said she had everything under control."

"I didn't mean to take anyone away from their work."

"It's no problem," Pearl said as she stretched on Lydia's front porch. "Besides I have some gossip I want to talk about."

Now Lydia smiled. "Come inside and let me get my walking shoes on."

Five minutes later, they were walking down the street toward the path that ran next to the river. Pearl kept the small talk flowing, and Lydia found she was grateful her brother had sent his wife.

Her friends had been pivotal in making her feel as if she'd slid right back into her life in Georgia. She'd arrived the night of the fire and stood there watching her dreams go up in flames with everyone else. No one made a big deal about seeing her there. It had been as if she'd never left. They started the process of relocating everyone and rebooking events the very next day. Again, they worked together as if she'd never left. Sure, they'd all taken their five minutes to hug and kiss her and welcome her back. But not once did they make her feel as if they had to coddle her, and that's what she had wanted. Well, except for her brother sending his wife to walk with her, but she'd forgive that.

Pearl talked until they were on the well-shaded path with the river running next to them.

"So, the gossip," she began.

"Oh, I've missed gossip. Todd is horrible with gossip. He never gave me enough," she said, but she did consider that there hadn't been any new gossip and her situation had been the gossip.

"Someone told someone who told me that they went by that new Greek place and saw Lydia Morgan and Phillip Smythe sitting in a booth by the window. Not only were they dining together, but they were sitting on the same side of the table next to one another."

Lydia let out a breath and looked at Pearl, who wore a wide smile, but kept her eyes forward.

"And this is your gossip?"

"Yep."

"You couldn't have just come out and said, what were you doing having lunch with Phillip?"

Their pace slowed and Pearl turned to her sister-in-law with sad eyes. "I thought it might be more lighthearted my way. I was wrong."

Lydia shrugged it off and picked up the pace, grateful to be out in the fresh air with her friend.

"Yes. The gossip is true. I dined with Phillip yesterday. I moved to his side of the table because we were sharing a gyro platter. And," she sighed, "it was awkward."

"I can assume it was. How did he talk you into lunch?"

"He didn't. I talked him into it."

"You?" Pearl had stopped and it took Lydia two steps to notice.

Lydia turned around. "Yes me. Why is that so weird?"

"Because as long as I've known you, you've run the other direction when it comes to Phillip. He comes around and you leave. You've never been nice to him, and yet he keeps coming around. So what gives?"

Lydia started walking again, and Pearl followed. She gave it a few steps, thinking about what she wanted to say.

"I've done a lot of therapy. A lot. My issues with my grandfather were dealt with. Learning that Tyson wasn't my real brother, but taken in by my parents, that was another thing to deal with and process, because I never had. Issues with trust and reliability of others, I dealt with that. In ways, what happened to me was eye-opening, though in the most horrific and traumatic way ever.

But I took the time to deal with everything in my life. And that included many therapy sessions dealing with my feelings for Phillip Smythe."

They stopped short of going under the bridge to turn around and head back. Pearl had been more than gracious to take a walk with her, but she had to get back to work. Lydia understood that.

"So you're seeing each other now?" Pearl asked.

"We had a meal together. One meal in fifteen years does not mean I'm dating the man. It means I didn't cuss him out or slap him. It means I appreciate that he worried about me. It means he's a decent human and deserves to be treated like one."

Lydia didn't look at Pearl's expression, because she didn't want to see shock, awe, or pity.

When they returned to Lydia's, Pearl gave her a hug that seemed to mend the parts of her that had frayed during the walk. When she went back inside, and began to lock herself in, she noticed that Pearl walked slowly to her car, waiting until Lydia seemed settled inside before she left.

Lydia was blessed to have a friend like Pearl. Even better—she was the sister Lydia had never had.

CHAPTER 4

*P*hillip shuffled papers across his desk. He wasn't sure he'd have accepted the role of captain had he known he'd be chained to his desk as much as he was. Report after report glazed his eyesight.

Then there was the fact that he'd had to go back twice to look for important details that he'd already gone over, because he wasn't focused at all.

Lunch the day before still had his brain in a fog. For fifteen years, Phillip had wanted nothing more than a little bit of Lydia's attention. He certainly never expected to get it.

Phillip eased back in his chair and rested his hands behind his head. Things had changed. Everything had changed.

There wasn't a night that went by where Phillip didn't have a nightmare about the day he pulled Lydia from that monster's house. Had Lydia not killed the man, he certainly would have.

But what had that done to her? She had taken a life. She had killed a man with her bare hands. She had saved other lives, including her own. Did that figure into her therapy? Did she understand the good that she did?

He had expected her to come back to Georgia a changed

woman. She had spent a year away from everything and everyone so that she could heal. There would've been no way to expect the moment he would see her for the first time would be when he went to tell her that her business was on fire. However, she was as cool and collected as she always was. She had asked him to wait a moment, gathered her purse, and walked out with him.

The drive toward the *Bridal Mecca* had been quiet, but she hadn't seemed anxious. Well, not as anxious as he thought she should have been. Instead, she sat quietly with her hands folded in her lap and had even asked him about his mother. When they'd reached the fire, she had gasped. As they stood there, he'd wrapped his arm around her shoulders—sure that she would push him away—but she hadn't.

There was a moment when she rested her head against him, and simply let him hold her.

Phillip understood that. Watching what she had built burn to the ground, she grieved. In that moment he knew she needed comfort. He hadn't expected her to continue her kindness toward him months later.

Phillip knew he wore on her nerves. And usually he didn't mind. It was a game to see if she would talk to him or run the other direction. He'd never cause her any harm, but he didn't mind getting under her skin a little bit. Once she returned from her sabbatical, he didn't feel like getting under her skin. In fact, he didn't know what he wanted to do. So, he'd just stayed away.

When she had invited him to lunch, he was sure he had stopped breathing. He waited, assuming he would wake up from a dream. For years, the only time Lydia Morgan would speak to him was in his dreams.

Phillip sat up and shuffled the papers on his desk one more time. It was useless to try and get anything done. Picking up his hat from the side of his desk, he put it on his head, stood, and walked out of his office.

He had made it past the conference room when Parker Davis

stood from behind her desk and hurried toward him. Her blonde ponytail swung behind her. Dressed in her uniform, gun on her belt, she looked tough as nails. Just like most police officers, Phillip knew there was a softness under the exterior.

"Headed out, Smythe?" she asked as she stood in front of him, only slightly taller than Lydia.

He winced when he realized he'd compared them, but he'd been doing that a lot lately, especially since Lydia had returned.

"Headed to the *Bridal Mecca* to see how the construction is coming. Then I have a meeting in the Mayor's office at one."

She nodded slowly, and he knew that the stop at the *Bridal Mecca* had caught her attention.

Her lips curled into a tight smile. "Will I see you tonight?"

Why did those words sock him right in the gut? "I'll call you," he said and watched as her tight smile puckered.

"Alright." Parker walked away, and he knew he'd hit a nerve.

Phillip pulled the keys to the cruiser from his pocket and exited the station as quickly as he could.

It had been fifteen years since he'd had a relationship with a woman, and he'd managed to get tangled up with Parker just three weeks before Lydia had returned.

Because of workplace rules, he shouldn't have even taken the invitation that had gotten him involved with Parker. But Phillip was lonely and heartbroken, and that's how things worked out.

Phillip opened the car door and slid behind the wheel. The July heat mixed with the humidity made it hard to breathe. The uniform he wore proudly constricted him.

As he pulled from the lot, he gave a small wave to the officers walking from their cars and into the station. Perhaps he'd take a long drive around the city, patrolling of course, just to calm his nerves.

Lydia had been on his mind all day, and now Parker was too.

One thing he knew about Lydia Morgan was that she was a strong and independent woman. Being assaulted and killing a man would burn in her conscience forever, but she'd use the tools she'd learned over the past year to lead a normal life.

Phillip drove the outer rim of the city and then worked his way down Main Street to check on the *Bridal Mecca*. Lydia's car wasn't there, so he parked and stepped out. Todd Walker had seen him and waved before walking toward him.

"It's going to be a while, but I feel like we're making progress," he said, tucking the clipboard he'd held in his hand under his arm, and shaking Phillip's hand.

"It'll be good to see it up and running again."

"I guess I'll have a job for life. When it burnt down Lydia bought more properties to accommodate the contracts we had. Pearl bought a building, which she plans to lease out when she moves back in here, too."

Phillip chuckled. "Those women own the whole town."

"It's pretty amazing." Todd wiped his hand over his forehead. "It would have been nicer to build in the winter. But there's a possibility it'll be up and running for spring weddings."

Phillip agreed with a nod. "She'll be happy to have everything back to normal."

"Did you discuss that over lunch?" A small smile had formed on Todd's lips and Phillip wondered if the whole town knew about his lunch with Lydia.

"No secrets here, huh?"

"Oh, you forget how tight-knit everyone is around here. I'm glad you guys are being friendly."

"She just needed a friend and I happened to be the first one around. I guess I was lucky."

Todd nodded his head slowly. "Lucky you. Well, I have to get back to *The Garden*. I'll see you around."

With that, Todd headed in the opposite direction, leaving Phillip alone in the parking lot considering how lucky he was when it came to Lydia—and how deceitful he felt pushing Parker away.

CHAPTER 5

*L*ydia set the alarm to her house and hurried to her car. The heat choked her as soon as she'd stepped outside. She'd lived in Georgia her entire life, so it wasn't anything new, but she realized that when she panicked, it got worse.

Before unlocking her car, she walked the perimeter and looked in all the windows. When she was satisfied that no one was hiding inside, she unlocked the doors.

Pulling open the door to her car, she slid in quickly, closed the door and locked it. Her next purchase was going to be a car that had an automatic start so she could cool it before she got into it.

Lydia started the engine and sat in the driveway, locked in her car, as it blew hot air at her. Eventually it gave way to cooler air and she took in three long and purposeful breaths.

When she'd left the first hospital, after her kidnapping, she'd sworn off any medications to help her deal with the anxiety that riddled her body.

Lydia Morgan feared nothing and no one, and that was how she wanted to live the rest of her life. But when she was home, her anxieties rose. After all, it had been in her own home that that monster had attacked her and kidnapped her.

She had plans to sell it, but she had a lot of other things on her mind too. The *Bridal Mecca* was one of them. Perhaps it burning to the ground had been a blessing. It had thrown her back into the society she loved, and pushed her to interact with her friends immediately. Otherwise, she might have stayed locked in her house.

Just as Lydia put the car in reverse, she saw the familiar patrol car make its slow drive down her street. Her heart raced even faster when Phillip pulled up in front of the house. She put the car back in park, opened the door, and stepped out.

Pushing her shoulders back, she put on her smile and watched as the lanky officer walked toward her.

"Out for a drive?" she asked as he pulled off his sunglasses.

"Yeah. Making my rounds." He hung his glasses from the front pocket of his shirt. "Headed out?"

"Making my rounds," she joked, but noticed that he didn't smile.

They hadn't had many civil conversations in fifteen years, so they weren't very good at it anymore. That was all on her, and hadn't she worked through that in her therapy?

Lydia leaned back against her car, which was still running. The heat from the metal seeped through her clothes, but she remained there, casually.

"Do you have time for a cup of coffee?" she asked. "We could go get one, or you could come in for one."

"It looks like you're headed out."

"Right. I have a meeting with Todd."

"I just talked to him. That's what he said. It looks like you're diving right back in. Busy as ever."

"Busy as ever," she repeated, keeping that smile on her lips that wanted to slip off and turn into tears. "I guess I'd better be going then. Maybe we could have dinner sometime."

She saw the shock register in his eyes, but his expression never changed. "Maybe we could. It'd be nice to catch up some more."

"I'm sure I'll see you around," she offered and even winked. Yeah, that had changed his expression.

"See you around," he said with a nod before slipping on his sunglasses and heading back to his car.

Lydia slid back into her car, and took another three thoughtful breaths. Again, knowing he wouldn't pull away until she drove off, she put the car in reverse and backed out of the driveway, waving as she passed him.

PHILLIP WATCHED Lydia stop at the stop sign and then turn left and disappear.

Leaning his head back against the seat, he took a moment to clear his head. What was he doing?

It had become habit to drive by her house three or four times a day. He'd expected that when she returned home, she'd call him out on it. But he didn't know how to react to the fact that Lydia that invited him to lunch, dinner, and coffee.

Rubbing his fingers over his chin, he gave some thought to how to handle his obsession with Lydia. He was well aware of the fool he'd made of himself since she'd walked out on him fifteen years ago. There wasn't a soul in town that didn't know how he'd pined for her and how she'd snubbed him.

A little part of him thought it might be nice to flip the tables on her. Maybe she was ready to pine for him, and he could ignore the signs.

No. He couldn't do it. The need to protect her and watch over her was stronger than it had ever been.

They weren't compatible. He knew that.

Phillip turned up the air conditioner and put the car in drive. He needed to get his head out of the clouds. Lydia tolerated him, and that had been all she'd ever done. Now it came with niceness and not the cold shoulder. If he kept coming around, she'd eventually hate him again. He wasn't sure that's what he wanted.

Maybe it would be best if he just moved on.

CHAPTER 6

*L*ydia was more comfortable when she was working. She sat in the small office of Pearl's bridal boutique talking venues with a bride. This had been one of the many changes they had made since the *Bridal Mecca* had burned down.

Instead of Pearl sending a bride to the reception hall to look around, she had Lydia meet the bride at the store.

Now that she had a few to choose from, she could get a feel for what the bride was looking for, and then they could visit the locations. With her mother wanting to retire, Lydia had taken on more employees, which meant more scheduling and paperwork. In the end, that was exactly what Lydia needed.

When the bride she'd been consulting with left, Pearl walked into the office and closed the door.

She occupied the chair that the bride had sat in, and crossed her legs, resting her manicured fingers on her knee.

"Did she sign?" she asked.

"We're meeting tomorrow at *The Garden Room*."

"I thought she'd go for that one. This is a good marriage. I think they'll be happy."

Lydia laughed. "You can always call 'em."

"I can. Sunshine is running out for subs. What do you want?"

Lydia wrinkled her nose at the thought of a sandwich. "I think I'll pass. That doesn't sound good."

"I can get you a sandwich, soup, order you a pizza." Pearl's voice strained. "Hell, I'll kill a cow for you if you want a steak. I just want to see you eat."

Lydia sat back in her chair and studied her business partner. "Is something wrong?"

"Yes. You're hiding in this office. You don't eat. You have your house locked up like a prison. It's been two months since you've been back, and though you seem like Lydia on the outside, I want to know what's going on inside."

Lydia bit down on her bottom lip when she felt it quiver. "Listen, if we have a problem, I'll work from another office."

"I didn't say *we* had a problem. I'm saying *you've* had problems. I know you are trained to deal with them. I know you're healing and you're doing an amazing job. But I'm sitting here with you every day, and I see this forcefield you're building. So if I'm any kind of a damn friend, or sister-in-law, then I'm going to ask some questions."

Lydia let her shoulders drop. "I'm fine."

"Fine doesn't cut it. Do you need a therapist here too?"

"I have one on speed dial."

"And that's enough?"

She gave it some thought. "For now." Lydia reached her hands out and took Pearl's, resting them on the desk, she held them. "I'm trying. I'm trying my hardest."

"No one said you weren't."

"Work makes me happy. It always made me happy. Home, well, that's another story."

"You're afraid of being alone at home?"

This would take a lot of strength, but hadn't that been what she'd trained for the past year? "Yes. I'm afraid of being home alone."

Pearl let out a hard breath. "Why didn't you tell us?"

"Because I have the tools to deal with it."

"You don't have to deal with it. That house is what should have been burnt to the ground. Not the *Bridal Mecca*," she chuckled. "Let's get you a new place to live. Hell, move in with us for now."

Lydia shook her head. "You have a family. I'm not messing that up."

"Messing that up? *Aunt Lydia is moving in*, will upset anyone?"

She smiled at the woman who was more than an in-law. "I want my independence back, and I just have to fight for that."

"Okay, well fight for it in a new house. Todd and Jessie like the real estate agent they worked with. I'm going to call her, make an appointment, and we're going to look at houses."

"We?"

"Yep. You're stuck with me. We're going to get you out of that house and into a new one."

Lydia pulled Pearl's hand to her lips and gave it a kiss. "I love you. I appreciate you looking out for me."

"I love you too. You're my sister. I have a back room of flat boxes, and I want you to put them in your car and start packing your house. I'll make an appointment and we will start looking for something new."

TODD HAD OFFERED to oversee the weddings for the weekend, and Lydia had taken him up on the offer. Since Pearl had talked about Lydia moving into a new house a week earlier, Lydia had been packing up her entire life with anticipation of finding a place and moving.

The house was stuffy, and the air conditioner was on the fritz. It would start, freeze the air, and then turn off completely. Lydia had suffered for two days before she finally opened the windows, one inch, and inserted wrenches, pipe, and wood in the window tracks to keep someone from opening them further.

She and Pearl had looked at three houses so far, but Lydia wasn't comfortable with any of them.

They had an appointment that afternoon to look at a townhouse. Though Lydia enjoyed her home, she wondered if having someone living on either side of her would be bothersome. Then again, maybe having someone nearby would be what she needed. Had someone heard her screaming earlier, the day she'd been assaulted and kidnapped, maybe they would have gotten to her sooner.

She pressed her fingers to her lips and waited until the vile churning in her stomach ceased before she took a breath and continued packing.

Elton John serenaded her from the speaker in the living room as she packed up her bathroom, leaving only daily essentials on the counter.

Then, the doorbell rang, and she froze.

Reaching for her phone, she brought up the app that would show her who was on her porch.

When she saw Phillip's face, her heart rate quickened, as it had before, and a smile came to her lips.

CHAPTER 7

*P*hillip wiped the back of his hand over his forehead. The heat in mid-July was sweltering, and he knew August would only make it worse.

He stood on Lydia's front step waiting for her to answer the door. The windows were cracked open and *Rocketman* blared from the speakers inside.

He was just about to ring the doorbell again when he heard the locks clicking from inside. A moment later, a smiling Lydia opened the door, and his heart danced.

The short mop of dark hair was pulled back in a headband, and she wore a pair of shorts and a tank top. The professional he was used to seeing had a sheen of sweat on her skin, and it stirred him up. Then he noticed the long scar that ran down her leg. The knowledge that she'd received that from the monster she killed stabbed at him.

She pushed open the security door. "I didn't expect to see you," she admitted.

"I'm sure you didn't."

The smile dissipated. "Nothing burnt down, did it?"

"No." Phillip laughed, and then adjusted the ball cap on his head. "Just came by to visit."

"Come in." She moved so he could pass by.

Phillip looked around the room. Furniture had been pushed up in a corner, and the dining room was filled with boxes stacked up against the wall.

"Going somewhere?"

Lydia locked the door behind him and moved to his side. It was then he could smell the vanilla musk she wore, and it made his head swim.

"Pearl convinced me to start looking at houses. So, I've looked at a few, and we have an appointment to look at another this afternoon."

"I think that's a great idea."

She turned to look up at him. "What are you doing here? I haven't seen you in a week."

Normally, he figured, she'd have been okay with that. "I just thought I'd stop and see how you were doing. That's all."

"Thanks. Let me pour us some iced tea."

She started for the kitchen, and Phillip realized that it had to be nearly ninety degrees in the house. "Why is it so hot? Don't you have air conditioning?"

"It's out. It'll kick on, freeze the place, and then take the rest of the day off."

"Maybe you should open the windows more. Get more fans," he said, and noticed the look of terror on her face as she handed him the glass she'd filled.

"I'm okay. Do you want to sit out on the back porch?"

Phillip nodded and followed Lydia out the back door, after she had unlocked the three locks that kept it secure.

The patio furniture had been pushed into a corner, just as the furniture in the house had been. Lydia set her drink on the small table and pulled two chairs on either side of the table.

Phillip waited for her to sit, and then did the same.

He sipped his tea, aware that she was studying him. "You haven't come around in a week. And since I've been home, I've only seen you a few times. What gives? Are you afraid of me?"

Phillip thoughtfully swallowed, not wanting to choke, but her question had thrown him off guard.

He took one more sip of his tea and set the glass on the table. "You didn't need me poking around. I figured I'd just step back a little and let you adjust. I've been in your way for the better part of fifteen years, you don't need me in the way now."

Lydia blinked her eyes as if tears might have been forming, but he didn't see any. "I'm sorry I was horrible for so long. That was unnecessary."

"To be honest, I was more used to that than you asking me to lunch and to sit for tea."

His honesty seemed to be humorous to her, and Lydia let out a laugh. "How did you put up with me?"

This was a question to be answered carefully. When he thought about the answer, it was because he'd loved her all those years. Her leaving him had never stopped that. But he wasn't going to say it like that.

"We're friends, deep down. You put up with that for a friend."

Lydia's eyes locked to his. "We were more than that."

He swallowed hard. "Once upon a time, we were."

Phillip picked up his glass as Lydia moved her chair so that she faced him. Surely, this was a tactic she'd learned in therapy, but he'd have rather her yell at him, or make a snide comment. He knew how to deal with that side of her.

"I spent a lot of time this past year working on us. You and me," she said, and Phillip felt himself hold his breath. "I needed to work through it."

"You and me? You and me were fifteen years ago. You up and left. I stayed. You came back. Fifteen years have passed, and we're good here." He'd heard his voice shake, and when Lydia reached for his hand and held it, he assumed she'd heard it too.

"A year, Phillip. A year I've worked on this in therapy. I can see it in your eyes, that you're more used to me snubbing you than you are with me talking to you."

"I'm a glutton for it."

She laughed again, and this time she intertwined their fingers. "I figured you were. You're trying to stay away, but you're still here, aren't you?"

"I should let you get back to packing."

"You should sit here and let me talk to you."

And he knew he should. Lydia didn't want to be alone, or she would have told him to leave already.

She only let go of his hand when her cell phone chimed and he took the opportunity to pick up his tea and drink it down.

Lydia let out a groan.

Phillip set his empty glass on the table. "Something wrong?"

"Pearl just texted. She has a bridezilla in her store and she's going to have to cancel on me for this afternoon."

"The appointment with the real estate agent?"

"Yeah." She studied her phone for a moment and then looked up at him. "I don't want to go alone. You wouldn't be available, would you?"

"You want me to go with you to look at a house?"

"Townhouse," she said, smiling. "But yes."

Phillip thought of his commitments for the afternoon. He'd been avoiding Parker as much as he'd been avoiding Lydia. But he'd told Parker to head out to his place after work. He figured that gave him a few hours. There was no reason he couldn't go with Lydia and make her comfortable.

"I could do that," he said, keeping his voice as steady as possible.

"Great. I'm going to go get a shower. Are you handy with air conditioners?"

"I could look at it for you."

"I'd appreciate that." She picked up their glasses and nearly skipped into the house with them.

Phillip sat on her patio for another moment to collect himself. He was in unfamiliar territory.

CHAPTER 8

The water was cool, and Lydia basked in it. Georgia summers could be exhausting, but she'd lived there her whole life, so she was used to it.

When she stepped out of the shower, and wrapped a towel around her, she felt the cool air from the vent. She smiled. Phillip must have gotten the air conditioner to work. She owed him one.

Taking the hand towel off the counter, she wiped the fog from the mirror and looked at herself.

Each time she did this, she pushed back her shoulders and took three long breaths.

Her hair was short, as it always was. When she'd returned to Georgia it had been longer, but she didn't like it. She'd lost some tone in her arms over the past year, but yoga had helped to rebuild it.

Lydia picked up the brush on the counter and ran it through her hair. After setting it back down, she took in one more long breath and held it as she dropped the towel to the floor.

After expelling that breath, she took three more and looked at her body. It would be easy enough to pass by mirrors or to always keep covered, but she didn't want to hide from herself. She'd never heal if she did that.

This was ritual now. This was staying focused and owning what had happened to her and accepting it. She didn't have to like it or appreciate it, but she had her life, and that was what was important.

As she did every day, Lydia ran her hands from her shoulders down over her breasts and held them there. She gave thanks for their health and pushed away any negative thoughts about her attack. Then she moved her hand to the scar that ran down her side. This took more than three breaths. The scar had been left from her attack. The bastard she'd killed had sliced his knife into her side before she'd taken that worthless life—she regrouped—before she'd taken that life. Hovering her hands over her belly, she closed her eyes and forced herself to open them again. Small marks wrinkled from her belly button outward. Three more breaths, and she closed her eyes again. A tear streaked down her cheek and she took three more breaths to bring herself back to appreciation.

Lydia moved her hands lower so that the hovered just between the gap in her thighs. She was grateful for every period. She was grateful for the times she was able to enjoy sex with men. She was grateful that she would be able to do that again—when she was ready.

Another scar raced down her leg, and she let her hand trail over it.

Turning her palms upward she looked at the tattoo that graced her wrist. It had been spontaneous, and meaningful. However, it might have been exactly the thing that drew that maniac to her.

She took three more breaths.

Tracing her finger around the tattoo, she thought of the meaning, and she closed her eyes. Acceptance was important in her recovery. No matter what, she was still in recovery mode, and would always be.

When she was done, she looked at herself in the mirror and silently affirmed love for herself. Moving forward would always be hard. The next man to see her body would ask questions. The next time she was intimate, it might hurt, or cause her emotional pain she wasn't prepared for. But by taking inventory each and every time she looked at herself, she was preparing herself for that.

There had been a million thoughts about moving on that had crossed her mind in a year. The Walker men were all spoken for, but she'd considered, before Todd met Jessie, that she'd sleep with him. Not because she loved him, but because she trusted him. He wouldn't let anything happen to her. She'd also considered a reckless one night stand that was over as quickly as it started. Maybe if she had reckless sex with someone she didn't know, and they left right after, she could fall apart and it wouldn't matter—but she would have moved on.

Then there was the thought that she could have sex with Phillip.

Three more breaths.

She'd loved Phillip, secretly, once. They'd been an item, but they'd kept it between them. He was rising in rank as an officer, and she still lived in her grandfather's home. Her grandfather thought as much of Phillip as he did of any of the Walkers. It hadn't been an option to be open about their relationship.

That was so long ago, but she still trusted him.

Three more breaths.

She shook her hair loose, as much to shake the thought from her head. She had an appointment to get ready for. Business was always first when it came to her life, and that wasn't going to change. The week would be filled with brides, meetings, commitments, and packing. There was no need to think about sex with Phillip as an obligation to herself. She didn't need sex.

Lydia picked up the towel and wiped it over her damp skin.

Tomorrow she would go through the same process. Some days it was easy. Others took a toll on her.

For now, she was going to keep breathing through it and enjoy her afternoon with Phillip. She was anxious for him to loosen up and be her friend. Too much time had been wasted resenting him. She just wanted them to be comfortable.

PHILLIP WAS in the kitchen when she emerged from her bedroom. He'd washed the dishes she'd had in the sink, and boxed up her bakeware.

"I hope you don't mind," he said. "I was trying to be useful."

"I don't mind at all. I figured if I was packed, I'd be more apt to find a place to live. This house..." she looked around but didn't finish her thought.

"It scares you?"

She shifted her eyes to meet his. "A little bit."

"You know, I have space at my place. I'd be happy to have you if you just need to get out of here."

Her heart squeezed in her chest. "That's very thoughtful of you. But I think I just need a fresh new start. A place where I can paint the walls a new color and know that nothing ever happened there."

She saw the flash of regret in his eyes, and she knew what he was thinking. The pang of guilt twisted her stomach. It was his house she'd walked out of fifteen years earlier after a fight. She'd left for a year, and never spoke to him or her family. As she'd stormed out of his house, she'd pushed the door open so hard it had broken off the hinges.

Three more breaths, she said to herself.

"I'm ready to head over to the townhouse. Do you want to meet me there? Or should we go together?"

"Are you okay to come home alone?"

Embarrassment heated in her cheeks. "Ah, you have other plans. I'll be fine. And thanks for the cool air. That'll make my night better."

"No problem. I'm sure it's a temporary fix, but..."

"Thanks the same. I'll lock up and we can meet at the townhouse."

CHAPTER 9

*L*ydia pulled up in front of the townhouse and Phillip followed. She parked the car and stepped out, taking in the sight. There were townhouses on both sides of the street, and ample parking. Each house, to either side of the one she was looking at, had planters of flowers and decorative wreaths on their doors. They looked well cared for, and that said a lot about the tenants.

The unit she was looking at sat in the middle of the row. Though she knew it was empty, it didn't look dilapidated. There was a small planter on the porch, no doubt kept by one of the neighbors.

As Phillip moved toward her, Lydia noticed the real estate agent walk across the street.

"Hello, Lydia," she called.

"Hi." Lydia waited for her to approach. "Jean, this is Phillip Smythe. He's an old friend. Head of our local police department."

Jean held her hand out to him. "It's a pleasure to meet you."

"Likewise."

"Old friend, huh?" she asked, and Lydia watched Phillip's cheeks redden.

"We've been friends for a long time."

"Great. I think you're both going to like this house. It's very cute." Jean moved past them and up the steps to the front porch. "These brick porches are so quaint. It's nice to have a place to sit and watch your neighbors come and go," she said smiling as she unlocked the door and pushed it in.

The moment they walked through the door, Lydia felt a peace she hadn't felt in any of the other houses. She welcomed it. Hopefully it was a good sign.

"The owners moved out a week ago, so it hasn't been sitting long. And they were original. These complexes are only a few years old."

Jean moved further into the room, which she had classified as the living room. There was a small alcove by a bay window, which she said would be a great place for a dining set.

They followed her to the kitchen, just beyond the living room, behind a swinging door. "The kitchen has all new appliances and room for an eating space in here as well. There is a door that leads to the back patio."

Jean walked toward it, and Lydia noted that it had a deadbolt, but it could use one more lock. Jean opened the door and they all stepped out onto the porch that overlooked the small yard.

"There is an alley behind the property and a one car garage. Such a great selling point for these houses."

Lydia wasn't sure she'd ever want to go through the alley to walk into the house, though she did like the thought of the garage. Perhaps it would be something she could work into.

As they walked back into the house, Jean walked them back through the living room to the staircase, and they followed her.

"There are two bedrooms upstairs. The master has its own bath, and there is another in the hallway." She turned into the larger of the bedrooms first. "This is the master. There is a walk-in closet just off to the side of the full bathroom."

Lydia noted the jet tub, and the size of the closet was ample enough to hold everything she'd ever owned.

Jean walked across the hall, peeking her head into the smaller bathroom before walking into the bedroom.

"This makes a nice spare bedroom, or home office."

Lydia looked at Phillip who smiled at her. "Work from home. There's something that seems appealing now."

He chuckled, but didn't say anything.

"What do you think?" Jean asked.

"It's lovely."

"It is. The owners are hoping to get it sold quickly, so if it's something you think you might be interested in, that might be a bargaining chip to getting a few dollars off the price. I'm going to see myself out, and let you two look around."

Jean passed between them, walked down the stairs, and out of the house as she'd said.

Phillip walked to the window, which overlooked the street, and leaned against the wall with his shoulder. "What do you think?"

"I think it's fantastic," she said enthusiastically. "It feels right. Does that make sense?"

"It does."

"It's like when I buy a building or a business. There's a gut feeling."

Phillip laughed. "Your gut is usually right."

Lydia walked back across the hallway to look at the master, and Phillip followed. She touched the walls and turned on and off the light in the closet multiple times. Then she moved to the tub. Oh, wouldn't that be delightful to soak away her cares in that?

"You'll never come out of it, will you?" Phillip's voice drew her attention to him. "You always loved to soak in the tub." The moment he said it, his eyes went wide, and she realized he'd eased too much for his own comfort around her.

"I do like to soak in the tub."

She watched Phillip cross his arms over his chest, and then move to tuck his hands into his front pockets.

Years ago they'd been comfortable in each other's presence. Now he couldn't stand still. For the past fifteen years, whenever she'd seen him, she'd walked away if she could, or made some snide comment. But now she didn't want to do that. She wanted to mend the broken heart of that seventeen-year-old girl who had fallen in love with the man who would protect the town, but he had to let her in—this new version of her.

"Do I make my decision now, or should I sleep on it?" she asked as she walked toward the closet and flipped on the light one more time.

"If it feels comfortable, maybe your gut is right."

Lydia looked up at the ceiling and noticed that the attic entrance was there. A cord hung down, and when she pulled it, the ladder that folded up inside came down at her. She stepped back out of fear it might hit her, and right into Phillip, whose arms wrapped around her to steady her against him.

When she'd caught her breath, she laughed. "I guess I have to be careful."

"I guess you do."

Her back was still pressed to his hard chest, and his arms still held her in place.

She gulped down the anxiety that had risen in her throat. "Can you add a lock to that opening? Something that would keep it shut, unless I unlocked it?"

"Yes," his voice vibrated against her.

Slowly, Lydia turned in his arms to face him. He didn't release her.

She looked up into those gray eyes she'd known so well—and still he held her.

Lydia pressed her hands to his chest. His heartbeat tapped against her fingertips.

The breaths that she always reminded herself to take were lodged in her lungs now.

Phillip's hands splayed on her back, and she lifted her arms to encircle his neck. Her fingers moved against his skin, and she rose on her toes to meet him, as their mouths came together.

The moment his lips touched hers, her senses exploded in delight. Butterflies took flight in her stomach and her head swam. His fingers pressed harder against her back, and she held on to him for dear life.

When his mouth opened to hers, she took what he gave. Pulling him closer to her, afraid to ever let go again.

It had been a lifetime ago and a lifetime in the making. She'd missed him. She'd pushed him away, and that was her mistake. In her heart she still loved the man she'd sent away. But here he was, holding her, kissing her, and protecting her as he always had.

"Are you still upstairs?" Jean's voice broke the thick air around them, and Lydia stumbled back, nearly falling over the ladder that dangled from the attic opening.

She could only manage one breath. "Yes. We'll be down in a moment. Just looking at the master."

"I'll wait for you on the porch."

Lydia held a hand to her pounding chest and watched as Phillip removed his ball cap and ran his hand over his hair. Then replacing his hat, he scrubbed his hands over his reddened face.

"I think you should buy the house," he said, his voice unsteady before he turned and walked back down the stairs.

CHAPTER 10

a few more moments in the master closet were necessary. *One breath. Two breaths. Three breaths.*

Lydia walked to the bathroom and looked at her face in the mirror. She looked petrified. She took three more breaths and then forced a calm smile to her lips before walking down the steps.

When she reached the porch, Jean stood from her seat on the step. "Well, what did you think?"

Lydia looked around for Phillip, and noticed his truck was gone.

"Oh, the house is great. I want to sleep on it, but I'll call you in the morning. I think it's perfect."

Jean's eyes lit up. "Wonderful. I think all people should sleep on a decision like this. I'll expect your call in the morning. And, yes, even though it'll be Sunday morning, I'll take your call. No rest for the motivated, right?"

Lydia nodded, having forgotten it was Saturday. "You're right. No rest for the motivated."

. . .

ONCE LYDIA DROVE AWAY from the townhouse, she headed straight for Pearl's store. She needed a few minutes with her computer.

Pearl was still dealing with the bridezilla when Lydia entered. She gave Pearl a nod and walked straight to the office, closing the door behind her.

The townhouse was on her mind, and she wanted to do some digging. Who had lived there? Who lived in the neighborhood? Were there any registered sex offenders? How often were the police called to the area?

The more she searched, the longer her list of questions became.

Thirty minutes later, Pearl walked through the door and closed it behind her. She fell into the chair next to the desk.

"That woman won't be married long enough to get the dress dry cleaned."

Lydia lifted her head from her work and looked at her sister-in-law. For the first time that she'd known her, Pearl looked frazzled, and that included the night of the fire.

"Bad news, huh?"

"Horrible. I added a surcharge to the dress of two hundred dollars."

"Two hundred?"

"She didn't even blink an eye. I think she's getting married to piss off her rich father. All she's managing to do is piss me off. Even Sunshine was in tears, and you know how she is," she laughed. "She spreads sunshine."

Lydia thought of the woman who worked with Pearl—Phillip's niece. The thought of his mere genetics had her stomach twisting.

Pearl inched in closer to the computer. "What are you looking for?"

"This is the townhouse."

"You still went to the appointment. That's good. I was worried you would cancel."

Lydia sat back in her chair. "Phillip went with me."

"Really?" Pearl's voice had risen in pitch. "That's interesting."

"He came by the house before you called. He fixed my air conditioner, too."

"Handy guy."

She knew the tone in Pearl's voice and she shook her head against it. "Don't get any ideas about me talking to him. I'm just trying to be nicer than I was in the past."

"I thought you were nice."

"To you," Lydia teased, and the tension in her shoulders began to slip.

"So how is he taking the nice Lydia?"

Lydia leaned in on her elbows and thought of the kiss—and then his retreat. "Not so well. I don't think he knows what to do with me. It's like he comes around just so I can snap at him and leave. But now I'm inviting him in for tea..."

"And for lunch."

Lydia laughed. "And for lunch. He acts all weird. I was still in the house and he left before I'd finished touring it." The story wasn't entirely true, but close enough.

"That's weird. Was he working?"

"No. Civilian clothes."

Pearl nodded. "Maybe something came up." She eased back. "Well, I'm ready to close up shop. It's been a long day."

"I'll wrap this up."

"You're welcome to stay as long as you want," she offered, but Lydia shook her head.

"No. No need to hang around. I'll head home."

Pearl left the office and Lydia finished up on the computer. She could do more searching on her laptop. The thought of the order of her house made her want to do anything but go home. But that's all that was left.

Phillip obviously didn't want to spend more time with her, so taking him up on the option to stay at his house was out. And now with Todd engaged, everyone was spoken for when the day was done.

She hadn't spoken to her grandfather in a year, so going out to his house was not an option. The only choice was to go home.

Her bedroom was still intact. She would take some drive-thru home and lock herself in her room with the TV on. Yes, that's what she would do.

PHILLIP DROVE straight home after he left Lydia at the townhouse. It wasn't the right thing to do, but his mind was so scrambled, he didn't know what the right thing was anymore.

He'd pestered Todd nearly every day for news on her while she was gone. Every week he'd gone to church with his mother and prayed for her speedy return. Now she was back—and talking to him—and he didn't know how to handle it. Oh, and then when they kissed...

Phillip gripped his steering wheel a little tighter as he pulled into his driveway.

It was everything he'd ever wanted, and he didn't handle it well.

A hot breeze was blowing and all he could think about was going inside and having and ice-cold beer. He hoped Lydia's air conditioner was keeping her cool.

He shook his head as he walked to the front door. Even when he didn't want to think about her, she was all he could think about.

Phillip turned when he heard the horn honking behind him, and Parker pulled her car in behind his.

She stopped, killed the engine, and stepped out of her car still dressed in her uniform. Like a child, she ran toward him at full speed, jumping up at him, wrapping her legs around his waist.

Her arms circled around his neck, and he had no choice but to hold on to her ass as she dangled from his body.

Her mouth came to his, hot and eager.

"Take me inside," she growled as her tongue skimmed his lips and her body ground against his. "I need to have this uniform taken off. I'm hot."

Phillip pulled her even tighter to him as he turned and managed his way to the door. This would make him forget about Lydia for a while. And that was what he needed. He needed to forget about her.

CHAPTER 11

The buzzing in his ears grew louder, and it took Phillip a moment to realize he'd set his alarm and it was going off. He reached across Parker's body and turned it off. She rolled toward him and wrapped her naked body around his.

"Good morning, lover," she whispered in his ear as she rolled with him to his side of the bed.

Phillip's head pounded and he squeezed his eyes shut against the sunlight that poured in through the windows.

Parker had called him lover, but he didn't much care for the term. But he supposed that was what he was—her lover.

In his mind, sex was all they had in common—and their jobs.

They never were in public together, and they'd never said the words *I love you*, mostly because he didn't love her. He enjoyed her company, but that wasn't love.

"Why on earth did you set your alarm on a Sunday?" she pressed kisses to his chest, but his head hurt too much to register it.

"I have things to tend to."

Parker groaned and rolled away from him, pulling the sheet up over her.

"I guess I'd better get up and head home then. I have nothing to tend to."

"You're welcome to stay here. I just need to get going," he said as he sat up and set his feet on the ground.

They'd started the night busting through his door and making it as far as the couch—then they cracked open the bottle of Jack Daniels. It had been ages since he'd drank off a mood. The sex should have helped, but it hadn't.

Phillip stood and gathered his bearings. When he looked back down at Parker, she'd fallen asleep. That was for the better he decided. She'd given him a good distraction for a few hours, but it hadn't been enough to wipe away the thought of Lydia's kiss.

His stomach churned and he wasn't sure if it was the liquor or guilt. Who had he betrayed? Parker? Lydia? Or himself?

He walked to the bathroom and shut the door. For a moment he propped himself up with his hands on the sink. When he lifted his head and looked in the mirror, he didn't even recognize the man staring back at him.

When had his hair gone so gray? And the bloodshot eyes look didn't make him look well. Who'd take him seriously in his job when he looked like he did?

Reaching into the shower, he turned on the water. He'd promised his mother he'd be at church before he went in to work. He supposed he had a lot to pray for—forgiveness mostly.

The moment he stepped under the hot water, his head cleared enough to make the decision that he needed to end this *thing* with Parker. It wasn't filling the part of him that needed filling. He wasn't sure who or how that need would be filled. But an affair with her wasn't it.

Pouring the shampoo in his hand, he lathered it up and ran it through his hair as he thought about ending things with Parker.

He had to be prepared for any kick back too. He was her superior, and their secret rendezvous were against the rules—and he was a rule follower. There could be serious repercussions if she turned him in. It was always funny how things like this would turn into a victim situation.

He didn't think Parker was like that. But that's where sex messed things up. He didn't know her well at all—and that wasn't how relationships worked.

Scrubbing his hands over his face, he heard his phone ring on the counter. Stepping out of the shower, water dripping in his eyes, he answered.

"Smythe."

"Good morning," Lydia's voice cheerfully filled his ear.

Phillip wiped the water from his eyes. "Morning."

"I'm buying that townhouse."

"At seven o'clock on Sunday morning?"

There was a pause. "Why did you disappear?" Her question took him off guard. This must have been the new Lydia—the one that asked questions instead of yelling or ignoring. He was used to the latter.

"Lydia..."

"Thank you for going with me. I just wanted to say that. It doesn't matter why you left. I made up my mind."

"Lydia..."

"Phillip, I'm sorry. I shouldn't have called. Too much time alone last night to dwell on it. I journaled six pages about how I felt about the house, and the kiss," she added, and his stomach tightened. "Listen, we need to not read into that. I've worked hard to come back home and make things normal. So if that's why you left, that's okay. I have the tools to move in another direction."

Because he couldn't focus, Phillip turned off the shower. "Maybe we can talk this out. Remember, I'm not used to you talking to me at all."

That brought a laugh, and he felt the tension ease. "You're right. I'm free today."

"I have some obligations, but I'll come by later."

"Thanks, Phillip," she said, and he gripped his phone tighter, desperate to keep talking to her.

"I could bring dinner."

"Oh," she sounded genuinely surprised by the offer. "I suppose that would be..."

"Did I miss shower time?" Parker pushed open the door and strolled into the bathroom not seeming to notice he was on the phone. "You still have soap in your hair. Why'd you turn the..." she stopped when she noticed the phone in his hand.

Phillip swallowed hard.

He heard the gasp on the phone. "God, Phillip. I didn't know —shit!" And with that the line went dead.

Looking at the phone, he set it back on the counter.

"Phil, I'm sorry," Parker said pulling a towel from the bar and wrapping it around her body. "I messed something up, didn't I?"

"I need to get finished and get going," he admitted, turning around and starting the water again.

"I'll get dressed and head out." He watched her walk away and didn't stop her. He didn't care to. All he cared about was straightening things out with Lydia.

As the water ran clear of shampoo, he thought about what he was going to say to Lydia. Did he owe her an explanation? They hadn't been together in years, and that had been hot and heavy, but short-lived. Since then she hadn't had time for him, so where did he owe it to her?

Letting the water spray his face, he decided he did owe it to her. His feelings for Lydia had never changed, and for years he'd tolerated her attitude. There should be some graciousness in his heart since she wanted to be nice. Perhaps there needed to be some ground rules.

There had always been respect for her, but now there was even more, especially after everything she had gone through.

Phillip turned off the water and reached for a towel. Lydia

deserved credit for putting her life back together. She'd been though tragic events which he'd never understand. They shouldn't have kissed, he decided. It had messed up his feelings and his head. No, his feelings were always the same when it came to Lydia Morgan.

CHAPTER 12

With hammer in hand, Lydia stood over the air conditioning unit wondering where she should hit it first. Phillip had fixed the damn thing, so why wasn't it working again?

Oh, hell. Phillip probably didn't know anything about air conditioners. Why should she think he fixed it? He'd never fixed anything.

Lydia took the hammer to the top of the unit and gave it a mighty swing. The unit kicked into submission and roared, but then stopped.

Letting out a primal groan, Lydia carried the hammer back inside with her, and locked the door behind her. She hated having to open the windows to allow any air through, but she'd have to do it.

Again, as she had the day before, she opened the windows an inch and secured them so they couldn't be opened further. She turned on every fan that she had in her possession, and this time while she was packing up the closets, she cranked up her stereo with Guns N' Roses, because it felt raw, just as she did.

As she filled boxes with linens and surplus toiletries, she thought about where she would put each item in the new house.

Jean had said she would submit Lydia's offer.

Moving on was what Lydia needed more than anything. She'd expected to come back from her sabbatical and everything would be normal. But that fire had changed all the plans. Her businesses had been uprooted and she'd been focused on rebuilding rather than moving on.

The new house would be the best start. She needed to focus on that. Anything would be better than living in her current home fearful and tormented by the memories.

Having unloaded the reachable shelves in the closet, Lydia pulled a chair from the kitchen into the hallway and stood on it to reach the top shelves.

She pulled down storage of keepsakes and Christmas decorations. Boxes that she'd packed when she left her grandfather's home only to be forgotten about were stacked at the very top.

It had been long enough, she wasn't even sure what was in the boxes.

Lydia made a stack on the floor, and when the closet was clear, she put away the chair and took the stack of boxes into her bedroom to go through them.

She carried the last box to her room when she heard what sounded like pounding on her front door, but the music was loud enough she wasn't sure that's what she'd heard. Pulling her phone from her pocket she turned down the music from the app she used. Then she brought up the camera from her doorbell.

Gritting her teeth, she watched as Phillip stood on her front porch in his uniform. The fact that the man had a gun on his hip didn't settle well with her, and since she'd done no wrong she didn't think he had any place in her house with a gun. Deciding not to answer the door, she turned the music back up from her phone.

. . .

PHILLIP STOOD on the porch waiting for Lydia. When the music had stopped, he knew she had seen him. However, when she turned the music back on, the heat surrounding him increased, as did his anger.

"Lydia!" He knocked on the door again. "I know you're in there. I need to talk to you."

Still she hadn't come to the door.

At what point would his knocking on the door be construed as too aggressive? As he reached his hand to knock again, he decided against it. Perhaps that would trigger her, and he didn't want to be the cause of that.

He'd probably been the cause of anguish to her in the past. He refused to be again. When she was ready, she would come for him.

Phillip turned and walked back toward his patrol car.

When he reached the end of the walk, he heard the music turn off. That had him turning around, just as Lydia opened the front door.

Instead of walking toward the house, he stood where he had stopped, and waited for her to speak to him.

"I didn't call for the police," she said from the door.

"I thought we were going to talk today."

"You said later, and that was before I heard what I heard."

Phillip rested his hand on the butt of his gun, which was habit when he was in uniform and having a conversation with somebody in the house while he stood at the street.

"What you heard was none of your business." He didn't like the tone in his voice, but it was the truth. Lydia had no jurisdiction over his life or what he did on his own time. Even though he thought that, he didn't believe it.

"I understand that it's none of my business. That's why I hung up the phone."

Phillip took a few steps toward the house, but noticed that

Lydia retracted the door just a bit. Those emotions he was afraid of, seemed to be triggered.

He stopped his advance and took his hat from his head, figuring it would be a little more personable.

"I think we need to talk. I think we need to hash out what happened."

"It was circumstantial," she said with a shaky voice. "We can just forget about it."

"Fine," he agreed and put his hat back on. "But I have the strangest suspicion you have a lot of things you want to talk to me about. Maybe we should start opening up that dialogue."

He noticed the door had closed even further. Now Lydia spoke through a slit where she held it open.

"You can come back. Come back when you're not dressed as a cop."

"Officer of the law," he corrected her statement mostly because it annoyed him to be called a cop.

"I don't care what you want to call yourself. I don't want you in my house with a gun."

And that, he thought had been the trigger. Seeing him in his uniform, his weapon to his side, had been why she hadn't opened the door. He couldn't blame her. He'd come to her home mad and armed. There was an ache in his heart when he thought about what had happened inside that house. The only thing he wanted for her was to get her out of it as quickly as possible.

"Okay." He lowered his hands to his side, making sure nothing came in contact with his gun. "I'm going to go back to the station, and change. I can't leave my gun in the car, so I'm going to make sure it's locked up. Then, I'm going to come back. And you and I are going to have a heart to heart."

She was silent for a moment, and then the door opened a bit wider.

"Fine. But you don't owe me any explanations."

"You're right. But as friends, we have things to discuss."

"I'll be waiting for you."

CHAPTER 13

*I*t had taken Phillip a little over an hour to go back to the station and change into his civilian clothing. He had locked away his gun and canceled his commitments. Then, he grabbed some lunch from a deli that he liked, and headed back to Lydia's house.

When he stood on the front porch this time, rock music still blaring from the speakers, he noticed the windows were cracked open. Dammit, the air conditioner must've given out again.

No matter how long it would take for her to get that new house, he had to get her out of this one. Aside from the mental torture, it had to just be miserable.

Chances of convincing her to stay with him were very slim, especially after overhearing Parker that morning while she was on the phone. He wouldn't apologize for it, he promised himself. He had nothing to apologize for. It was his love life, and Lydia had nothing to do with it.

The moment he reached the front door, the music stopped. He didn't knock, or ring the doorbell, but instead waited for her to come to him. After a few seconds, he heard the locks on the other side of the door open.

"I brought us some lunch. I hope you don't mind," he offered.

Lydia opened the door, and he could see that the heat inside the house was taking its toll on her. Her hair was damp, as well as the front of her shirt. Again, she had on a short pair of shorts which showed the scar on her leg. He did his best to keep his eyes averted from it, knowing that if she saw him looking at it, it would make her uncomfortable.

"I didn't mean to be so nasty to you earlier," she said regretfully as she opened the door fully so that he could step inside. "I guess some things just set me off. I'm working on that. I hope you'll be patient with me."

He would be.

Her new approach had obviously been part of her therapy, and wanting the best for her, he promised himself he would be patient. Chances were, much like giving up alcohol or drugs, dealing with trauma in one's life could come with a jagged emotional state.

Phillip stepped through the door and stopped to wait for her to lock it again. The temperature inside was drastically higher than outside, with the fans only blowing the warm air around.

"I take it my air conditioning fixed didn't last?"

"No, but I don't think that's on you. I think that's the unit."

"Perhaps we should take this somewhere else. Without the windows open, I'm afraid you're going to pass out from the heat."

"You probably think I'm some sissy for keeping the windows as sealed, but I just can't open them all the way."

That set his pulse on fire. "I would never think you're some sissy for taking precautions in your own home. I know what happened in this house. I would not ever want something like that to happen again."

The moment the words were out of his mouth he regretted them instantly. He had no right to mention the house and what happened there. If he thought the gun had triggered her, that had to set her off with a vengeance.

Instead, she began to cry.

The last time he had seen her cry she was seventeen and it was the day that she disappeared all those years ago. He couldn't afford to let her out of his sight at this point. What if she ran away? He didn't want to chance it.

Phillip sat the bags of food on the floor and pulled her to him. Lydia didn't pull back or argue. She rested her head against his chest and let him in envelop her in his arms.

"That was insensitive. I didn't mean to upset you. I think I'm a little worked up, and this heat isn't helping," he apologized.

"I must come across like a maniac. I hate being afraid. I've never been afraid."

"You have every right to fear. Jesus, you spent an entire year away learning to cope with this. You couldn't imagine that you would come right back and jump into your life without fear, did you?"

She stayed where she was, her head rested against his chest. "I wanted to. I wanted everything to just be the same. But nothing is the same."

Phillip placed his hands on her shoulders and eased her back. "The way I see it, we can either sit in my truck with the air conditioner running, or go to my place. It's much too hot in here to think. Seriously, I'm afraid you're going to pass out."

"No. I'm fine here. Maybe we can get the air working again. Could you look at it? I took a hammer to it, but..."

Phillip sucked in a quick breath. "You took a hammer to it?"

"I was mad. I was in a mood," she quickly corrected. "I don't think I hurt anything, maybe."

Wiping the sweat from his brow, he pushed a smile to his lips in hopes of creating a calm between them. "Okay, I'll go look at it. But if I can't fix it, we need to make other arrangements."

Lydia stepped away from him, and he noticed her fists balled up at her side. "I don't have any other arrangements. Everyone has other commitments. They have their families. Nobody needs me in their home being babysat."

"And you know that's all bullshit. Every person in your life would take you in, no matter how many people were in their family. I'd venture to guess you've had some invitations and you turned them down. Those who haven't yet invited you probably assume you're doing fine because you're always fine, and you tell them you're fine. And if I'm not mistaken, I offered you a place. You are welcome in my home."

He knew the heat was getting to her, as her shirt grew wetter and her hair damper. The pink in her cheeks grew rosier as she lifted her eyes to meet his. "You did invite me into your home, but what you didn't mention was there were other people in your home. People who share your shower with you and I have to assume, your bed," she said with a bite of anger.

There was no finessing around it now. Heat or not, they were going to have this conversation. He reminded himself again that his love life was none of her business. But he wanted to be a friend. He spent the last fifteen years being her verbal punching bag, he saw no reason why he couldn't continue to be that.

"Fine, do you have something to say about it? Let's get this out in the open."

CHAPTER 14

The heat was nearly unbearable, but Lydia couldn't—wouldn't—think of leaving her place when she wanted to have a fight. In the end, she knew how it would go down. She would lash at him for what she'd heard on the phone, and he would leave. Then she would be alone again. That was what she wanted, wasn't it?

Was it?

Her head swam with the anger that was building in her, and the heat that surrounded her. The moment he left, she was going to fill the bathtub with cold water and get in. This was probably horrible for her health.

Phillip picked up the bags he'd brought in and took them through the kitchen.

"Unlock this door," he demanded, standing in front of the back door. "It's at least ten degrees cooler outside in the sun."

He was right. She unlocked the door and watched as he walked out and began to set up the little table they'd used the day before.

Lydia went back into the kitchen and poured them each a

glass of iced tea, with lots of ice. Just the coolness from the glass helped to bring down her temperature.

By the time she reached him on the patio, he had set up their lunch and appeared to be calm. That was all in a day's work for Phillip, she decided. He didn't deal with the rational folk, no, he had to keep his calm while non-law-abiding citizens attacked him.

He was good at his job. He managed to keep bringing her into reality, and she needed that. Coming back home had been a lot harder than she'd imagined.

Lydia carried the two glasses toward Phillip. She handed him one, and then sat with hers still in her hands, cooling them.

"Thank you," he said before taking a sip. "You always could make great tea."

The compliment eased the ache in her chest. "Thank you. And thank you for lunch." Her voice was more controlled now and she felt calmer being outside.

Phillip had divided up the larger sandwich he'd brought and dumped out a small bag of potato chips between them.

Lydia took a chip and sat back in her chair. "While we're passing around the thanks, I want to thank you for looking after me."

"I would always take care of you," he promised.

"I know." And she did know that, and hadn't she exploited it for years? He'd have been there for her no matter what—no matter when.

"Why don't you stay with your mom?" he asked as Lydia took another chip.

"Mom took care of me for a long time in Hawaii. She fed me. Nursed me when I'd get too low. She needs a break."

"She said that?"

"No. I say that. I can't imagine what seeing me that low did to her. I don't want to make her go through that again. I want that pillar of strength to be there when I need it. And I want her to look at me and be proud."

"She'd be that way no matter what."

"You're right. But this is how I choose to handle it."

Phillip nodded slowly as he picked up his half of the sandwich and took a bite. Lydia looked at the simple meal before her, but just the sight of it made her stomach ache. She wasn't hungry. But she knew before Phillip left, he'd make her eat her share. He was there to push her to be normal, whether he knew that was his role or not.

She picked up her half of the sandwich and took a bite to satisfy him.

Setting the sandwich back down, she followed the bite with a sip from her tea, just as Phillip lifted his glass to his lips.

"So, who is she?" Lydia asked and watched as Phillip's eyes grew wide. "You know, the woman who was missing out on shower time this morning."

Phillip swallowed two large gulps of tea before he lowered the glass, his eyes still fixed on hers.

"The line repeating in my head is that none of this is your business." He held up a hand when she'd taken a breath, to stop her rebuttal. "But we're friends. I'll answer."

He took another sip from his tea, and then set the glass on the table.

"The woman you heard was someone who I've been seeing for a few months. Nothing serious. Just some company."

The ache was back in Lydia's chest, and she bit down on the inside of her cheek just to keep her teeth from chattering.

"Nothing serious? But she sleeps in your house? In your bed? She joins you for showers, but she's nothing serious?" With every question, the pitch of her voice grew higher.

"We're only having a conversation, remember? I'll go if you want to attack me."

She nodded. No, she didn't want him to go. She needed him there. "I'm sorry."

"Don't be sorry. God damnit, stop saying you're sorry. You've never been sorry about anything in your life."

His anger was fueled by hers, so she tried to reel it in. "I'm sorry now. You have no idea how sorry I am about things that have gone on in my life. It's okay for me to say I'm sorry."

"Well, you're not going to use it with me. Not when you're sorry for me getting worked up over your questions. Or sorry that I'm here, or whatever you want to back down from. You want to know about my love life, then I guess I'll tell you."

"But really it's none of my business."

"No, it's not. But once upon a time you were my business, and then you pushed me away for years. So you can see where I get a little heated over you giving a damn."

"I give a damn because you kissed me a few hours earlier."

Now his entire face had gone red, and she was sure it wasn't from the heat. "I kissed you? Oh, sister, you were as engaged in that as I was. It just happened. It was the heat of the moment, and it just happened. Never in my life did I think that it would, but it did. So yes, I kissed you and then had a woman in my bed last night. Is that what you want to hear? Is that what you want to know?"

His voice had risen to a shout and tears rolled down Lydia's cheeks. Her head swam from the heat and anger. No, she didn't want to know he'd slept with anyone. Perhaps she'd hoped that since she'd walked out on him he'd only pined for her, because that would have made her feel better. But it wasn't true. He'd moved on from her, no matter how much he came around.

CHAPTER 15

*A*nd now what was he supposed to do with her sitting across from him crying? The crying thing was new. The yelling, he knew how to handle that.

Phillip moved from his chair and knelt down in front of Lydia, who had buried her face in her hands.

"Look at me," he said as softly as he could. "Look at me."

When she lifted her eyes, they were red from tears. Her hair was wet from sweat, and she looked miserable.

"Friends. We have to remember we're friends. If this is hard on you, tell me, and I'll stop coming around. But I won't give up on you. I'll just send over your other friends."

Lydia wiped away the tears on her cheeks. "I need you. You're the only one not walking on eggshells around me. My feelings got hurt. That's all."

He understood that and now he'd be more sensitive to the fact that she had feelings—because before, he wasn't sure she did.

Phillip held his hand to her cheek and she pressed her hand to his.

"Phillip, I trust you."

Why had she said that? He kept his eyes focused on hers. "You can always trust me."

"I know. And right now, I need someone I can trust. I need someone I can trust with my feelings. Someone I can trust in my house when I'm not in the same room with them." She slipped her fingers between his as he continued to touch her cheek. "At some point, I'll need someone I can trust with my body."

"Lydia..."

"Hear me out." She pulled his hand from her face and linked their fingers. "I don't want to be afraid of intimacy for the rest of my life. I rather enjoy having sex and being in a relationship."

Those words stabbed his heart. They'd had a relationship once. One that was full of love and that intimacy she spoke of. They were young, oh, so young. They'd kept it secret. Her grandfather didn't approve of him, and at the time, Lydia couldn't separate the woman she wanted to be from her obligations to her family, nor should she have needed to. Though she was nearly eighteen, she was just a child, and he at twenty-one wasn't any more mature.

So what was she trying to say to him by telling him he was the only person she trusted? Did she need to work through the issues with him? He wasn't sure he was mentally adjusted enough to accept being used in such a way. His feelings for Lydia Morgan still ran too deep, even if he was sleeping with Parker.

Lydia guided his attention back to her.

"I'm not asking you to give up the relationship you're in."

He let out the breath he realized he was holding. She could see into his soul—still.

"I'm not asking you to love me. I'm opening up to you. I trust you. And until I find someone else I can fully trust, I'm going to be emotional around you. I'm going to cry. I'm going to yell. I'm going to lock you out," she said laughing. "I need you, Phillip Smythe. And since I know you will keep coming around, I'm going to count on that."

"I will always come around."

"You've spent the past fifteen years proving that."

"But you've pushed me away for fifteen years. Why am I the one you want to count on?"

Lydia moved to the edge of her seat so that they were nearly nose to nose. "You were the first man I ever shared my body with and my heart with. I trusted you then, and you've proven I can trust you now."

"Then come home with me. Stay with me until you're ready to move. Get out of this freaking heat."

"You're in a relationship, and I won't tread on that."

Phillip eased back on his heels. "I don't love her, Lydia. Much like you, sometimes I need to have intimacy too."

"You're using her?"

"Hell no. But it's only physical. I don't love her." He moved in closer to her again. "I've only ever loved you."

Her eyes went wide when he said it, and her hands raised to his cheeks. Leaning in, she took his mouth with hers, and once again, he couldn't stop the need to kiss her back.

WARMTH, which wasn't associated with the rising heat outside, shot through Lydia as Phillip's mouth worked against hers. She was hungry for him, and by the way he responded, he felt the same way.

Why had she spent the past fifteen years hating the man? The demise of their relationship hadn't been his fault. Lies, secrets, and running had been the demise. But she didn't want that anymore.

Phillip pulled her to her feet, his mouth and tongue still entangled with hers.

What did she want from him? Did she want what they'd had fifteen years earlier? Was she just looking for that healing moment when someone she trusted touched her?

Phillip's hands pressed against her lower back. She'd raised her arms to wrap around his neck and held on for dear life.

She wanted him to touch her. She needed to know that having a man's hands on her body was tantalizing, and not fearful. Could she go through with it? The last man to touch her had done it with a vengeance. He'd held her down, choked her, hit her, and taken what she refused to give.

With the memory of it filling her head, she held on tighter to Phillip hoping that the memory of what they'd had, and the pleasure of what they were doing, would push that fearful one away.

The moment his hands cupped her ass, she gasped, and he stepped back.

"I'm sorry," he said panting for air. "There are lines. I don't..."

"Shhh." She pressed her lips to his again. "I need this. I need you."

The kiss was different now, and she could feel his trepidation resonate through his body.

It was then they heard the doorbell, and Lydia stepped back.

Each of them sucked in a breath.

"I'll see who that is," she said, moving from him.

Phillip caught her hand, and when she turned toward him, she thought he might apologize. But he didn't. Instead he gave her hand a squeeze and bit down on his bottom lip.

He wasn't done either.

CHAPTER 16

*L*ydia let Phillip's hand fall as she entered the sweltering heat of her house and walked toward the front door.

Rising on her toes, she looked through the peephole in the door to see who was there. She would have looked at the app on her phone, but the walk across the house had given her a moment to catch her breath.

Standing on her front step were Pearl, Audrey, and Gia.

Lydia let out a long breath. Any other time she would have been thrilled to see the women she loved standing on her porch, but today, she'd been content doing what she'd been doing.

Lydia unlocked the many locks on the door and pulled it open.

"Get your purse and let's go," Pearl enthusiastically said.

"I'm not ready to walk out of this house." Lydia motioned to her sweat stained clothes.

Pearl fanned herself. "What the hell is going on in there. I think it's hotter inside," she said, obviously having been hit with the air from inside the house when Lydia had opened the door.

"Put on a hat and some clean clothes. You're coming with us."

"And what are we doing?"

Audrey smiled as she pushed her sunglasses up on top of her head. "*Abby May.*"

"You're taking me to a spa?" she asked, recognizing the name of the day spa in town.

Pearl nodded. "Yep. But it's not just a spa day. Abby called me yesterday and said that when the *Bridal Mecca* is back up and running, she'd like us to consider leasing her a space. She wants in. Can you imagine if we had something like that for the brides? It's a win, win."

It was hard not to catch Pearl's enthusiasm.

Pearl's attention shifted behind Lydia, and her smile adjusted accordingly.

"Hey, Phillip."

Lydia turned to see him near the kitchen. He lifted a hand and waved.

Pearl leaned in. "Did we interrupt anything?"

It was normal for her to ignore Phillip when others were around, so she easily responded, "No."

"Well, then, let's go."

Because of the heat in the house, Pearl and the girls had opted to wait for her in the car with the air conditioner running.

Lydia took a quick, and cool shower, but agreed to just throw on a hat and get to the car as quickly as possible.

Once she was dressed, she hurried out of the bedroom, ready to lock up the house, only to find Phillip outside hovering over the air conditioner unit.

"You're still here," she said.

He lifted his eyes, which were sad now, to her. "I was trying to get this running for you. Since I can't convince you to stay with me."

Guilt swam in her belly. She'd thrown a fit over him sleeping with someone, and then kissed him again. Everything she was doing was selfish, and he didn't deserve this, but she needed him.

"I'm running out with the girls."

Phillip stood and walked toward her. "Do you trust me to stay and finish this? At least we could cool down your house."

She had said she trusted him, and she did.

"I do trust you. I'll get you a key."

Lydia moved back into the house, and retrieved her keys from her purse. When she handed it to him, she lingered her hand over his.

Looking up into his eyes, she drew in a breath. "Lock up when you're done. I'll come by your place later and get these."

It was a loaded sentence, and the way his eyes widened she knew he understood. She wasn't going to leave things the way they had. She wasn't done yet.

LYDIA HAD WAITED for more questions as to why Phillip was in her house, but no one said a word. They chatted, as they would on any other given day, during the drive toward the spa. Once they were inside, they were each given a list of services they would receive, and Abby had given them a tour of her facility.

She wasn't looking to move out of her current spa, but instead open another location. Lydia loved her enthusiasm and knew right away they were kindred souls.

After the tour, each woman undressed in their own private room, and put on a lush robe. They met back again in a secluded waiting area with plush chairs, fruit infused water, and a selection of snacks.

Audrey and Gia were escorted out, leaving Pearl and Lydia alone in the room.

"I didn't ask if you wanted to do this, because I didn't want to give you a chance to say no," Pearl said as she sipped on her infused water. "I know that having someone touch you is going to be hard."

"I'm working on letting that go."

"Well, I asked that our massages be done at the same time, in the same room. But I can ask them to separate."

Lydia was grateful for her sister-in-law. She understood her as well as if they'd been blood relatives.

"You're very thoughtful."

"I can't imagine what goes through your mind when you know someone will touch you. But I think this will be a good thing."

Lydia swallowed hard. She'd blindly followed Pearl to the spa, not giving any thought to someone touching her, perhaps because her body was still sizzling from Phillip's kiss. But Pearl had given thought to it.

Lydia reached her hand to take hold of Pearl's. "I appreciate this. I want to try and move forward."

Pearl smiled. "Don't get mad, but I took liberty to tell them you had scars." Lydia tensed, and Pearl leaned in. "I saw the one on your leg. I don't assume that's it."

"It's not."

"Okay then. Step one, right?"

"Right."

Pearl lifted Lydia's hand to her lips and kissed it just as a big sister would. "And then when you are all relaxed, you're going to tell me what the hell is going on with you and Phillip Smythe."

Lydia pulled back, but Pearl's smile remained.

"Me and Phillip?"

"Yeah, and don't tell me nothing. I am a woman who had a hot and lovely affair with the man I married. So I know what it looks like when you're interrupted."

As the door opened and the masseuses came to retrieve them, Lydia pursed her lips. Nothing *really* had happened with Phillip. But she wasn't sure she wanted Pearl to know anything at all. There was still a lot she needed to process when it came to Phillip—and some of that was fifteen years in the making.

CHAPTER 17

*P*hillip spent the better part of an hour trying everything he could to make the air conditioner work. He was handy enough, but not completely mechanical. So, he did what he could do, and then he called Jake Walker.

Jake arrived at Lydia's house with a toolbox and an iPad.

"What's with the iPad? Are you going to watch movies while you help me?" Phillip asked as he led Jake through the house and to the backyard.

"The entire world is on the internet, including how to fix your air conditioner. So don't give me any crap. And why the hell are you at Lydia Morgan's house? Where is she?"

He could answer all of it truthfully, but he had to question, why he was really there too. He was there because he couldn't stay away from Lydia. It was as if she were his drug, and always had been.

"I've been checking up on her. I just want make sure she's adjusting well. I can't imagine coming back from what she went through only to have her business burn to the ground and have to start all over again."

"Hey, man, I didn't mean anything by it," Jake said as if he were threatened. "I've seen her around you for years, she doesn't have much to say to you. So imagine that I'm just a little bit surprised that you called me to help you and you were in her house alone."

Phillip deserved that. He was being a standoffish asshole. He took his ball cap off his head and ran his hand over his damp hair.

"The girls came and got her for an ambush spa day. At least that's how I understood it."

"Good, she could use something like that." Jake knelt in front of the air conditioning unit, with his iPad to his side. Phillip watched as he connected it to his phone's hot spot, and then looked up a YouTube video. After a few moments watching over Jake's shoulder, he too had a better idea of how to get started.

Jake took the side of the unit off, and begin to take out screws and make adjustments.

"Have you ever fixed an air conditioner before?" Phillip asked.

"I have built over thirty cars from the ground up, this can't throw me off too bad. Although, I think she's going to need a new one. Anything I do here is only going to be a temporary fix."

"She just needs something to get her through the heat right now. She won't open her windows, well not more than an inch. She's living in this house in terror. The least we can do is try to get her some cool air."

Jake lifted his head and exchanged looks with Phillip. "In terror? Seriously, she's that scared to be here?"

Phillip wished he hadn't said anything. It wasn't his place to say anything.

"I'd be terrified. I know what happened in this house. I know what it looked like after he took her." Thinking about it made Phillip sick to his stomach. "Don't you dare tell her I said this out loud. Right now she's speaking to me, and she seems to need the comfort of our friendship. She'd kill me if she knew I was saying this."

Jake nodded. "I won't say a word, but thinking of you and Lydia as friends is a long shot, don't you think? The woman hates you."

One thing about Jake Walker was he didn't hold punches. Yes, Phillip could concur that he, too, had thought Lydia Walker hated him. However, after the past two days, he wasn't so sure.

Needing him to touch her, made sense to him. They did share history, and she was comfortable with him once.

"All I know is the woman needs comfort. She needs things to be what they were before, well, before that maniac took everything from her."

Jake nodded in agreement. "We're all here for her. She knows that right?"

"Yes, she knows. She knows just how blessed she is."

WITHIN AN HOUR JAKE had figured out which fuses to replace, and which wires needed a little TLC. Another hour and one trip to the hardware store later, Lydia's house was finally cooling.

Jake had left, and Phillip walked through the house checking every room. She had nearly boxed up everything she owned and pushed the furniture into the corners. How could that possibly have given her any comfort?

He noticed that she had a stack of boxes on her bed. She wouldn't even be able to stay in her own house and sleep in the bed the way it was. He decided to take it upon himself to stack the boxes neatly against the wall. She could go through them at a different time.

As he picked up the last box, the bottom began to give out. He managed to kneel down to the floor just as the bottom opened. A sense of deceit filled him, as he saw the contents spilled onto the floor. It was a box full of her memories, and right there amongst the knickknacks and the keepsakes was a picture of him and Lydia.

Phillip sat on the floor and held the photograph. They were both so young.

She had hair past her shoulders, and those ratty old cut-off's that she loved to wear with her white Keds and her plaid button-up shirt. She looked as though she had walked out of some eighties movie. But that was her style.

He, on the other hand, never had any style and the picture was proof of it. More lanky as a young man than he was now, just into his twenties, he towered over Lydia. His hair, then dark brown, was full and shaggy. That was evident by the amount of it that hung out of his ball cap. The photograph was taken outside of his mother's house, and he remembered the day. It wasn't long after that photograph was taken that Lydia disappeared. Perhaps, deep in her therapy she was able to address why she left him—why she left everyone.

What would it take for her to tell him why she left? He'd been prepared for her to go away to school. He'd even considered marriage if she stayed. Always the plan had been to get her out of her grandfather's house the moment she turned eighteen.

He must've meant something to her for all those years if she kept that picture. Now, curiosity had him wondering what else was in the box.

No. He was an officer of the law, and this was trespassing. She had invited him into her home, and trusted him to stay there. She said nothing about going through her personal belongings.

Phillip managed the knickknacks and keepsakes back into the box, and secured the bottom. He set it on the stack with the other boxes and left the bedroom, closing the door behind him.

CHAPTER 18

*L*ydia was enjoying the moment. Soft music, diffused lighting, and essential oils filled the air. Pearl was on the table a few feet away, and each of them seemed to be in their own world.

She appreciated what Pearl had done, thinking about her situation and being there in case it became too much.

Having a massage wasn't what she considered moving past having someone touch her, but it was helping. There was nothing malicious or sexual about it. Lydia was free to enjoy the peace of it.

An hour and a half passed, and Lydia was sure she could've laid there for another hour. Soon, she and Pearl were whisked away. Pearl was sent to a facial room, and Lydia met up with Gia in the pedicure room. Luckily, Pearl had never brought up the subject of Phillip.

"I think this will be a fantastic addition to the *Bridal Mecca*," Gia said.

"I agree. But if all the businesses go back into the same building, where will we put it?"

Gia gave her a smile that told her they had already discussed it at some point.

"We were thinking that, upon remodel, what if we added second story offices to the top of the building? Ella could easily relocate upstairs, it would give you more space in the hall, and we could lease out the other offices. You could even make it an open floor plan, with private offices and have one of those shared workspaces."

Gia's eyes had lit up when she spoke about it.

"And we're sure all the businesses want to come back, right? I mean Pearl is doing great in that building she bought. Jessie's studio came together nicely. Audrey's stylists are all over the city..."

"And everyone wants to be back where we were. Lydia, we're a family there. You are part of that family."

She knew that, and that was making her transition back home easier.

"I think we should have lunch tomorrow, all of us at Pearl's, and discuss it."

Gia reached for her hand and gave it a squeeze. "I think that sounds like a perfect plan."

PERFECTLY PAMPERED, and relaxed to the core, Lydia sat in Pearl's car, numb. The breeze from the air conditioner blew on her dewy skin as she admired the shimmery pink that had been painted on her fingernails.

Pearl dropped Audrey and Gia off at their homes before heading toward Lydia's house.

"I know this sounds weird, but since we're on this side of town, would you mind dropping me off at Phillip's?" she asked and instantly felt the gaze Pearl focused on her as they waited for the stoplight to turn. "He has my keys since he locked up my house."

She heard the hum that came from Pearl. "You just want me to stop by his place so you can get the keys. That's what you mean?"

Lydia swallowed hard and rubbed her silky smooth hands together. "No. If you wouldn't mind dropping me off, that would be great."

Pearl nodded and turned in the opposite direction of Lydia's house. "You know, we never..."

"No. We never discussed it, because there is nothing for you to know. I'm giving Phillip some gracious attention as part of the therapy I worked so hard on. He's been nice enough to help me and be there for me. But there's nothing between us."

"Nothing?"

"You don't believe me?"

Pearl held up one of her perfectly manicured fingers. "If you say nothing, then I know there is nothing. I'm just thinking that he came around for years, and you paid him no attention, and now you're giving him plenty. Don't you think that's going to send the wrong signals?"

Lydia turned her attention out the window. No, she wasn't worried about sending the wrong signals, she'd been straight forward with what she needed.

PHILLIP STOOD IN HIS DRIVEWAY, his head under the hood of his truck. After he and Jake had worked on the air conditioner, he felt the need to do more manly tasks. He'd headed home and cleaned out his truck and changed the oil. Now, as he filled his washer fluid, he heard the sound of a car coming to a stop in front of the house.

Wiping his hands on the rag in his back pocket, he turned his hat back around, and walked around the truck.

It was Pearl's car stopped at the end of his long driveway.

Phillip leaned up against the side of his truck and watched as Lydia climbed from the passenger's door.

A lump formed in his throat. She was there—at his house.

Her hair was pulled back with a band, and her face was clean of any makeup, but it was rosy, and he liked that. She looked healthy and relaxed. Pearl had done a good thing taking her to the spa.

"I came for my keys," she said, but Pearl didn't drive away.

When she drew closer, Phillip looked back toward the car, and then to her. "Kinda thought you might stay a moment."

"That's my plan. Go tell my supervisor that you'll take me home. She thinks there's something wrong with your truck."

He grinned, and without even getting close to Lydia, he passed by her and walked to Pearl's car.

The window on the passenger door rolled down, and Pearl, looking as fresh and relaxed as Lydia, smiled up at him.

"She says you have her keys."

Phillip gave her a slow nod. "Jake and I fixed her air today."

The quizzing smile she'd given faded into gracious. "Thank you. I was worried about her."

"I am too. And hell, she seems to be letting me fuss over her, so I'm going to."

Pearl turned in her seat. "I'm worried about that too."

"I've been fussing over her for years. Why worry?"

"Because she's letting you."

"I know. Jake pointed out that she hates me. I'm fully aware of the volcanic eruption that could happen at any time. I'll never hurt her, Pearl. You know that."

Pearl let out a long breath. "Yeah, I do know that. But she might hurt you."

And that, he thought, had been the norm for the past fifteen years.

"I'm a big boy. I can take care of myself." He paused a moment. "She looks relaxed."

"She made it through the massage, a manicure, pedicure, and a facial. I think that's great progress."

Someone had touched her, and that had been very important to her. "That is. I'll get her home. I'll even have her call you when I do."

Pearl smiled widely. "Don't let her forget to do so."

Phillip backed away from the car, and Pearl rolled up the window as she gave Lydia a wave and drove away.

Phillip turned to walk back toward his truck, but stopped to take in the sight of Lydia who had climbed up on the front bumper and was looking at something—it didn't matter. She was there, and comfortable to be with him at his home. He would tread lightly. That eruption could happen at any moment.

"I didn't know you knew anything about trucks," he said as he walked toward her.

"Can't say that I do. I just wondered what you were working on." She jumped off the bumper and stood in front of the truck.

"Jake came over and helped me fix your air conditioner, and then when I got home, I changed my oil. I was feeling awfully handy."

"You got Jake to come over to my house and fix my air conditioner?"

Phillip nodded. "Seemed like the smartest thing I could do. He's the only guy I know that understands engines, or motors. He got it working."

"I owe you guys."

"I hope it's still working by the time I get you home. How was your spa day?" He asked as he wiped his hands on the rag in his pocket.

"It felt like an ambush, but it was great. I had a facial, a manicure, pedicure, and a massage. I cannot believe I got a massage."

Phillip closed the hood on the truck and turned to her. "That's a big step. I know that was important to you."

"It is. It was. It was a start," she said moving toward him. "I'm still anxious to see how it will go being touched, well, in other ways."

Phillip rubbed his hands on the rag he still held because they had become sweaty. Though he loved having Lydia want him around, and wanting him to be the man who touched her, he just wasn't prepared. How was he supposed to go from fifteen years of silence and hate, to being the object of her affection?

Sure, he had told Pearl he was a big boy and he could handle a heartbreak, but could he? Lydia Morgan had broken his heart once. Could he handle it if she did it again?

There was also the case of Parker Davis. She had left that morning when she interrupted his phone call, and he hadn't stopped her. But at some point they were going to have to have a talk. If he slept with Lydia, there was no going back. After that, he would never want another woman in his life.

CHAPTER 19

*L*ydia wondered if she had made a mistake. Before she had left her house, she and Phillip had been entangled in something that could've gone farther. When she gave him her keys, she had hoped he understood her innuendo. In fact, she was very sure he had.

Standing in his driveway, she wondered why he was so nervous. Then again, why wouldn't he be? How would she feel if she had spent fifteen years trying to talk to someone and all they did was ignore her? She deserved it.

The problem with those fifteen years was she was the only one that knew why she went away. Well, her, her brother, and her grandfather. Upon her return, she turned her back on Phillip. There was no need to. She should've told him all the things that she needed to tell him, but she didn't. She'd been too young to understand it all—anger and resentment were easier emotions to control. So she spent years treating Phillip like a second-class citizen.

She looked at the tattoo on her wrist and thought of its meaning. There was so much more to what she wanted with Phillip than just a night with someone she trusted. Once upon a time she loved the man. She would've given up everything for him, of course in the end she folded under her grandfather's rules. She had been young and foolish. They both had been young and foolish. But they weren't anymore.

Lydia watched as Phillip tidied up his driveway, putting away his tools and locking up his truck. She had to consider that he had told her he'd been with another woman the night before. Relationship or not, she knew Phillip well enough to know that he didn't take that lightly. No, he wouldn't touch her if somebody else was in the picture.

"If you wanna finish this up, I can have Pearl come back and get me. I didn't even consider you had other things to do today."

Phillip looked up and those gray eyes looked sad. "This was just occupying my time," he admitted. "I set out some steaks. I thought I could grill them up. I'm not much of a whiz when it comes to salads, but I did get some vegetables. Maybe you could do something with that."

He'd planned dinner. That was something. Lydia pushed a smile to her lips and agreed with a nod.

PHILLIP CLOSED UP HIS GARAGE, and invited Lydia into his home. He never thought she'd set foot into his place, but he was grateful that she had. Nerves fluttered in his stomach, much like they had when he had first met her. So much had happened since then.

"I have a bottle of wine, or I have beer. Would you like one?"

Lydia pulled out one of the stools that Phillip had around the island in his kitchen. She sat down and looked around.

"I'd much rather have a beer than a glass of wine, if you don't mind parting with one."

Phillip opened the refrigerator and pulled out a can. He opened the top and handed it to her. She laughed when she read the label.

"I'm a partner in this brewery," she looked up at him. "Did you know that?"

He nodded as he pulled out a can for himself, opened it and took a long pull. "I had heard that. It's not bad."

She was smiling now, though he couldn't quite decipher the look in her eyes. Hell, he only bought the beer because she owned it. It was okay, but it wasn't a Bud.

Pulling the steaks out of the refrigerator, he set them on the counter. "I don't marinate them. Just some salt and pepper, little bit of butter in the end. Does that suit you?"

"I think that sounds delicious."

"The vegetables for the salad are in the refrigerator. Knives are in the drawer, and the salad bowl is in the cupboard. I'll go get this started."

Lydia watched him as he let himself out the back door.

He needed a few more moments alone with his thoughts. He had her in his house. There had been an invitation on his part. Having her as a guest would keep her near, and keep her safe. But he couldn't make her stay.

However, having her safe was only feeding *his* soul. He had to contend with what *she* wanted.

It wasn't that he didn't want that, he did—he always had, but it was sudden, and still so strange that Lydia wanted to be around him.

He certainly wasn't going to push her away. When she'd come home, he'd given her space. He'd stayed clear for nearly two months. In that time, she'd decided she wanted him around, so he had to consider that. But still, after fifteen years of wanting nothing to do with him, he was adjusting.

LYDIA MOVED about Phillip's kitchen as if she'd been there hundreds of times. It was like they thought the same. She knew where everything because it was where she would have put it.

Did that mean something? She chuckled to herself. All it meant was that Phillip was practical, and she already knew that about him.

While he cooked the steaks and wrapped his head around her being there, she chopped up a beautiful salad and made a garlic butter for the steaks. There were a few pieces of bread that were a day from expiring, but she salvaged them and popped them in the oven to broil them for garlic bread.

She'd found the plates, silverware, and even some linen napkins. She gathered everything and carried it to the porch so they could eat on his patio.

"You don't have a table out here?" she asked and his head shot up, obviously unaware she was standing there.

"What? No. I don't eat out here much. I don't have people over—often." She heard him choke on his words, and she knew it had triggered the thought that he'd had a woman there the night before.

Lydia forced the thought from her head. "I'll set the kitchen table then."

"Did you make garlic bread?"

"I did."

A smile curled the corner of his mouth. "These need a minute, and then they'll need to rest a few minutes. I'll be in shortly."

Lydia turned back to the house and set the kitchen table. He was nervous, but by the end of the night, she would get what she wanted—needed.

CHAPTER 20

*P*hillip carried the plate of steaks into the house and stopped when he saw Lydia sitting at his kitchen table. She'd set it and lit a candle. He didn't even know he had a candle. It wasn't anything fancy, and someone must have given it to him for Christmas in a gift swap or something. None the less, he couldn't believe how homey—and romantic—it was.

"I didn't think I was out there that long," he said as he walked toward the table.

"I was occupying myself," she admitted. "I hope you don't mind that I was in your cupboards."

"My home is your home," he offered, and he meant it.

Phillip set the plate on the table and sat down across from Lydia who lifted her beer and took a sip. Why was it that watching her do that stirred him up?

As he lifted one of the steaks and slid it onto her plate, she smiled at him. She really did look good.

"You look relaxed."

"I am," she said as she dished them each out a scoop of salad and a piece of garlic bread. "I didn't want to go with them. I was enjoying what we were doing before, but I'm glad I went. The lady that owns the spa wants to put a satellite location at the *Bridal Mecca.*"

Phillip picked up his knife and began to cut into his steak. "But if you all move back in, the building is full."

"Right. Gia said they'd all been talking, and since we have to rebuild, maybe we could add a second story of offices. That would move Ella up, give me an office out of the hall, and we could rent private office space. Then we could adjust the sizes of the spaces, and it would fit a small spa."

There was a twinkle in her eye when she talked business, and he found that it did something to him to watch her plan. It had always been that way, even if he did it from afar.

"That sounds adventurous."

"I think it'll be a nice new start."

"And you're into new starts, aren't you?"

Lydia lifted her can and took another sip. Her eyes had gone darker now and he knew he'd stirred up that conversation about her needing him without having meant to.

When her beer was empty, Lydia stood and walked around the table. Phillip eased back in his seat when she came to stand next to him.

In a fluid motion, she straddled him on the chair, and instinct had his hands coming to her hips to hold her in place. Something told him they weren't going to finish their meal.

"I want to pick up where we left when the girls came to pick me up," she whispered as she leaned her head toward him and pressed a kiss to his neck. "I can't stop thinking about it. I trust you."

"Lydia..."

She eased back and looked him in the eyes. "Please," she said with desperation dripping from her voice.

Phillip studied her eyes as he raised his hand to her cheek. Then, he pulled her to him and took her mouth.

Lydia's arms wrapped around his neck and he stood, holding her around him. Without leaving her mouth, he carried her down the hall to his bedroom.

This wasn't how he'd wanted to do this, or how he'd imagined it a million times. But Phillip couldn't fight her advances any further. He was human, and his feelings for Lydia were too deep to ignore.

When he reached his bedroom, he pushed open the door with his elbow, his mouth still on hers. Lydia's legs were tight around his waist, and her arms held her to him as she worked her mouth against his.

He managed them to his bed, and when he laid her back, her eyes opened wide, and she pulled from him.

"Where are your sheets?"

Phillip winced as he stood. Pressing his fingers to his eyes, he sucked in a breath. "I took them off the bed this morning."

"Right." Lydia let out a long breath. "I'm not the first woman you've had in here this week."

He turned from her. "Lydia, maybe this isn't going to happen. Not that I don't want it to. God knows you're all I've thought about for fifteen years."

He heard her moving, and a moment later she was standing behind him, her arms wrapped around him, her cheek pressed to his back.

"You thought about this?"

He turned, capturing her in his arms and holding her. "You gave up on me. I didn't give up on you."

"I didn't give up," her answer came quickly and now she turned from him. "I didn't leave you on purpose. Shit happens, Phillip. I was young. I didn't have all the answers."

"What are you talking about?"

She lifted her eyes to him. "I'm not ready for that yet."

Phillip narrowed his gaze on her. "Tell me again, why me?

Where does it lead us in the end? Why do you want me to be the one to carry you through this part of your therapy?"

Tears began to fill her eyes and her lip quivered. "Because I love you."

CHAPTER 21

$\mathcal{P}$hillip sucked in a breath, and then another. He'd waited to hear her say those words to him again, but had long ago given up on ever hearing them.

"Lydia, don't say that if you don't..."

She cut him off with her finger to his lips. "I do mean it. I've worked to get to this moment all year, Phillip. I've journaled it. Done therapy sessions over it. I've prayed, cried, broken down over it. I can't go on like we did for fifteen years, but you have every right to push me away."

He reached out and touched her cheek. "I don't want to push you away. I just want to know what happened. I get that we were young and stupid. But we wanted to make a future for ourselves."

"I also worked on explaining it all to you, but I know at this very moment, I'm not strong enough. But I will be."

He had to accept that. What choice did he have if he wanted her in his life—and he wanted it.

She lifted her chin and smiled. Shadows covered her now, as the sun began to go down. "Now, where are your sheets?"

Phillip cringed at the very thought. There would always be Parker to deal with, but that was for another time too.

"If we're going to do this, you deserve better. I'm not going to make love to you on my bed where you know damn well I had another woman," he said and the words twisted inside him. "And I won't take you home. If I have any say in it, you'll never sleep there again."

Lydia pressed her hand to the one he held on her cheek.

Phillip sighed. "Let's take you home and get you a change of clothes. I'm going to take you to a nice hotel. You deserve the best if we're going to do this. You might hate me tomorrow, but at least I'll have given you a nice memory."

Her lips parted and he could see the tears pooling in her eyes. "I've never really hated you."

He wasn't sure about that, but he'd hold on to the words *I love you.*

WHILE LYDIA PACKED HERSELF A BAG, Phillip made arrangements at the nicest hotel in town. Because she deserved it, he arranged for champagne and strawberries in the room. They might need some room service as well, since they'd forgone dinner.

Phillip took a moment to call in a personal day as well. If this actually worked out, he didn't want to have to leave her bed and run to work. Besides, it would give him one more day away from Parker before he'd have to talk to her.

Lydia returned from her bedroom with a bag. She had changed her clothes and curled her hair.

"The boxes I had on my bed were moved," she said.

"I did that. I thought you wouldn't be able to sleep there with them scattered there. I hope you don't mind. I didn't go through anything."

A smile formed on her glossed lips. "I appreciate you thinking of me. And thanks for having Jake out to look at the air conditioner. It feels nice in here."

"Maybe it'll hold up until you get the place sold."

"I think I'm going to rent it," she said as she reached for her purse on the kitchen counter and pulled it over her shoulder. "It'll be a good source of revenue. And it'll give me reason to gut it and make it shine."

"You're incredible, do you know that?"

The smile she wore grew bigger. "You think that?"

"I always have."

Lydia bit down on her lip. "I'm sorry we went so many years not talking."

"Let's forget about those. I made reservations and there is a nice hotel room waiting for us. Are you sure you want to spend the night with me?"

Lydia set her suitcase down and walked toward him. Lifting on her toes she pressed a gentle kiss to his lips. "I've waited much too long for this. I'm very sure this is what I want."

WITHIN THE HOUR, Phillip was pulling up in front of the hotel, opting for the valet parking for his beat-up old truck.

"You booked us a room here?" Lydia asked, her eyes wide as they pulled in.

"Oh, just wait. You deserve the best."

He caught the smile that lit up her face. It was almost nine o'clock. He'd gone all out on the few hours that they would be at the hotel, but like he'd said, she deserved the best.

Lydia wandered the lobby as Phillip checked in. He confirmed the details he'd asked for when he'd booked the room, and was given two key cards.

When he turned, Lydia was standing near the window of the small jewelry store looking at the display.

"See anything you like?" he asked as he came up behind her and she leaned into him.

"So not my style. But I was thinking about how classy Pearl

always looks with her bracelets and rings. She has a natural beauty that I just don't have."

"I wouldn't say that."

She turned to look up at him. "You think I'm beautiful?"

"From the very second I ever laid eyes on you. Pearl may have some kind of grace, but you're youthful, energetic, full of amazing ideas and ambitions that I'll never understand. You're vibrant, full of life, and compassionate to others. You're..."

She reached up, locking her arms around his neck, and pressed a kiss to his lips. "Take me to bed."

As they rode the elevator to the room, Lydia held a hand to her jumpy stomach. She'd spent nearly a year in therapy dealing with what she'd done to Phillip over the years. Two months home, and she'd taken their relationship from zero to one hundred in a matter of days.

The moment that wicked man had broken into her house and started his attack on her, and she'd closed her eyes, it was Phillip's face she saw saving her. She'd focused on it, meditated on it, and journaled about it. There had been no doubt that when she returned to Georgia, she had wanted Phillip to be the first man to touch her and help her wash away what had happened.

It was about to happen, and wasn't he making it an event?

She had figured they'd have ended up in her house some-where, maybe on the floor, since she'd pushed away all her furniture. His house would have been ideal, but he was right, taking her where he'd been with another woman the day before just seemed like a bad soap opera. That part should have bothered Lydia more, but she was too focused on what she needed to care that someone else might get hurt.

This was something special. And even if she fell apart in his arms, she would always remember what he did for her.

When the elevator door opened, Phillip escorted her down the hall, his hand on the small of her back.

He stopped in front of the room and unlocked the door with the card.

"This is it," he said without pushing open the door. "Are you sure?"

Lydia looked up at him. "Absolutely."

"Give me your suitcase."

She rolled it toward him, and he pushed it into the room, and dropped his bag alongside it. Then he scooped her up in his arms and carried her over the threshold.

CHAPTER 22

*I*t had been an impromptu thought, to carry Lydia over the threshold, but Phillip understood what this night meant to her. Nothing was about him tonight. He needed to make her feel welcome, safe, and loved.

No matter what happened when they woke up, she'd been planning this night with him—he'd never understand why—as therapy to move on from what had happened to her. The way he understood it, this would be like her first time all over again.

He'd been there for that too.

When he set her on her feet, she pressed her face into his neck. Was she crying already?

Easing her back, he looked into her eyes. They were moist with tears.

"We can stay up and watch TV all night and order room service if that suits you better," he offered and she choked out a laugh.

"I just saw the champagne and strawberries."

Phillip turned his head to see the arrangement on the table. "I want this to be a perfect night for you. You have it built up in your head, and I don't want to let you down."

She wrapped her arms around him and laid her head on his chest. "I'd saved that bottle of champagne. Do you remember it?"

Phillip held her to him tightly. "Oh, I remember it. The first alcohol I ever bought. I hadn't known you saved it until those thugs broke into the reception hall."

Now she pulled back. "What are you talking about?"

Shit! Todd hadn't mentioned it. "The guy that caused the fire, he broke into the liquor closet. Todd said they broke the bottle that you'd explicitly told him never to open, serve, or move."

"I thought it just went up in the fire," she sighed.

"You have no idea how much it meant to me to know that you still had it. When I saw it on the floor, my heart ached."

"Did you tell Todd what it was?"

"No. Only you and I knew about it. I think they only speculated about us, I don't think anyone but your brother really knew. And I don't suppose he knew we'd planned to get married and drink that champagne."

And wasn't that a secret they held too? They had planned to elope the moment she turned eighteen. Her grandfather had meddled in their relationship hard enough, and they were going to run away. But then she disappeared.

Lydia looked around the room he had arranged for them. Not only had he arranged the champagne and strawberries, but a bath with salts had been drawn, and there were rose petals on the bed. Small tea lights flickered in the bathroom and on the nightstands.

"Is this the honeymoon package?" she asked as she lifted her arms around his neck again, and he pulled her in tight.

"It is. You deserve it."

"The candles are fine, but no lights, okay?"

"Whatever you want."

She bit down on her lip. "I have some scars."

"Okay."

"I don't want to think about them, and I'm not exactly ready for you to see them. I'm too conscious of them. I know everyone has seen the one on my leg, but no one has mentioned it."

"Whatever you want from me, need from me, I'm here. And, Lydia, I hope this is all you want it to be, because I made myself a promise, no one after you. I've pined too long to have you in my life, and here you are. The past two days have been a whirlwind ending me up right here, and this is where I've always wanted to be. I'm not saying that you're bound to me forever. I understand what this means to you. It's a process. But for me, it's a celebration of you coming back to me, speaking to me—needing me. You telling me you loved me, well, that was probably the best thing I've ever heard. I won't hold you to it, but..."

"Phillip, I do love you." She pressed a kiss to his lips. "That's been my problem all along. I went away and didn't know how to accept you back in my life. This time, I'm not going to do that. This is it for me, too. No one after you."

That was all he needed to hear. Phillip hoisted her to his hips and carried her to the bathroom where he set her on the counter, the candles flickered around them.

With her still in his arms and his breath held, he began to unbutton her shirt, and she pulled open the snaps on his. When she pressed her hand to his chest, his heart raced even faster.

She looked up at him. "Are you nervous?"

"More than the first time we ever did this. Do you remember it?"

She nodded. "In the barn on my grandfather's ranch. We stayed there all night."

"I was scared to death he would shoot me."

"He might have tried," she teased with a kiss. "But I'd never let him hurt you."

Phillip slid her shirt from her arms and noticed how her shoulders drew in. It wasn't personal, he reminded himself. Next time, and he decided there would absolutely be a next time, she wouldn't have to worry about scars. He wanted her to be comfortable around him, but he understood the process.

As she pushed his shirt from his body, he released the clasp on her bra and watched as she eased it off in the flickering candlelight. Lydia sucked in a breath but kept her eyes on him.

They were going to be alright, he thought as he took her mouth and they continued to undress one another. Again, he lifted her to him and carried her across the room to the large jetted tub where rose petals floated on a fizzy scented surface. As he set her down, his fingers skimmed her side he noted the scar and his stomach tightened. He'd touch it again, and they'd discuss it in time. But for now, this was about making up for the past fifteen years, and helping her forget what that maniac had done to her.

She loved him, and didn't that make everything in his life righted? Now, to right her life.

CHAPTER 23

She had let Phillip touch her.

And she had cried.

Lydia now lay with her head rested on Phillip's chest as he softly snored, and she smiled.

From the moment he'd unbuttoned her shirt, until the moment she opened her eyes as the sun peeked through the window, she'd run the gamut of emotions.

Every kiss, every touch, every moment of exploration was healing, and somewhat new. It had been a long time since anyone had given her that kind of attention, and she'd been right, it could only have been with Phillip.

The darkness shrouded her secrets, and her insecurities. But they'd both promised that they'd never have someone else after the night they spent, so what did that mean for them?

She still had things to work out with him, and maybe he would be the one to run after that.

He stirred and his arm came around her. Phillip kissed the top of her head, and she sighed against his skin.

"This has to be the best morning I have ever had," he whispered into her hair. "I never thought I'd do this again."

Lydia lifted her head and pressed a kiss to his neck and then to his mouth. "Thank you."

Phillip slowly opened his eyes. "Why are you thanking me?"

"Because when I couldn't handle it, you let me cry. When I needed a moment of wild, you let me take control. You touched me, and I didn't cringe. I needed this for so many reasons, and you made it so much more than I'd expected."

"I told you. You deserved the best."

Lydia rolled until she straddled him. Looking down at his sleepy, handsome face, she knew this was how she wanted to wake up for the rest of her life. Too many hateful words had been said between them, fueled with her breath. The need to tell him she wanted him there forever were stuck in her throat.

She noticed that in the sunlight, he was looking at her. And though he didn't seem surprised by her body, she did notice that for an instant his gaze lingered on the small lines around her belly.

But when he lifted his eyes back to hers, they were only full of love.

A small smile formed on his lips and he took her hand.

"One question. Why the tattoo. I thought you never wanted one of these. You swore they were trashy," he reminded her and she looked at the tattoo she'd had inked a year ago, right before she'd been kidnapped.

And infinity symbol with a small heart—the meaning went deep and he needed to know.

"I'll tell you sometime."

"Now is a good time. We've done a lot of work in the past few hours."

They had, and she felt so free, she didn't want to ruin it.

It was then her phone rang, and then his rang.

"What time is it?" she asked as she scrambled from the bed to find the phones.

"Eight-thirty," he said as she tossed him his phone and answered hers.

"Todd, what's up?" she asked.

"What's up?" Todd's voice was raised in her ear. "Where in the hell are you? We had a meeting at eight o'clock. You're not at your house, but your car is. You're not at Phillips' where Pearl left you. His car is gone. You're not anywhere and you haven't been answering your damn texts! We have everyone looking for you. Where in the hell are you?"

Lydia looked at Phillip who was talking down an equally frantic Pearl on his phone.

"I'm sorry."

"You don't get to just say you're sorry. Not after the year you've had. You're on constant watch because we love you, and you need to understand that."

"I do. I just..."

"You just what? You lost track of time? You took off with Phillip, because I find that hard to believe."

"Todd," she said smoothly and softly. "I'll be there. I need an hour."

"I have shit to do."

"I know. And I appreciate you and I love you. And I'll explain this when I get there."

She heard him groan and watched as Phillip disconnected his call.

"One hour. If you're not here, I'm sending an official search party out for both of you, and I'll press charges against him if I have to."

"No need. I'll be there. Thank you."

When she disconnected her call, she looked at Phillip walking toward her.

"They're a little mad," he said, and she let out a breath.

"I didn't expect this."

Phillip reached his hand out to her and pulled her to him. "Screw them. Now they know you're safe. They know you're with me, and I want to take a shower before I face the firing squad with you."

She chuckled. "You're going in with me?"

"Of course I am. There's no need for you to go alone."

"That's not fair to you."

"It's not about fair, it's about us." He ran his hand over his hair. "So, let's put this on the table. Was this one night? Was this just so you could move on and forget it? Was I just someone you trust and not attached to anyone? Or is this more?"

Lydia swallowed hard. "What do you want?"

"No, you don't get to turn it on me. I told you where I stand. And I don't think I've made it a secret how I feel over the years. I've always been present, you're the one that pushed me away, and that's fine. I got used to that. But things changed in the past few days, and I'm not okay with it being a roll in the sheets and that's it. Now, we've used words, we've reminisced, and we did our share of making love last night. But this has to be your decision. I told you, there'd be no one after you, but I can't just be that friend, or that once upon a time. I'm all in, or I'm out—for good."

Her heart hammered in her chest. "I told you, I love you."

"You did. And you know I love you. I always have. But when we walk out of this hotel room together, we either have to walk away hand in hand and let everyone see it, or we have to walk in two directions."

Their affair had been a secret all those years ago, and her hatred of him had only fueled rumors that there had been something. Hatred, that was such a strong word when it came to what she'd really felt for him. It had been regret and shame, not hate. It would be a big step to move forward and walk through the front door of Pearl's shop hand in hand. It would take more courage than it had to let Phillip touch her.

"So?" he interrupted her thoughts. "What's it going to be?"

One breath. Two breaths. Three breaths.

"They need to know what's happening here. If you'll have me, and love me, I'd like to feel out those plans we had so many years ago," she finally said.

She watched as his eyes grew moist with tears and he batted them away. "Wow," he said on a breath. "That's even more than I could have asked for. Okay, then we walk in there unapologetic."

"Right."

"They're going to fire questions at us with cannons."

"I'm prepared."

"Then let's get in that enormous shower and get ready to face them."

Lydia agreed realizing he would see her fully now, in the light. It was time be honest with her friends and family as well with the man she'd always loved.

CHAPTER 24

$\mathcal{C}$ompletely out of selfish need, they'd made love one more time before they checked out of the fancy hotel room and headed toward Pearl's store.

On the drive, Lydia had fielded calls from Todd, Pearl, and Tyson. Phillip, however, let his phone go to message when he'd seen that it was Parker that had called.

He'd tend to her, but first, he would make a statement with Lydia by walking through the front door of Pearl's store hand in hand with her.

This adventure was swirling in his head at a million miles an hour. She'd said she wanted to feel out those plans they'd had all those years ago—and those plans had included marriage and happily ever after. Neither of those things had happened, and now here they were, embedded as an item, and he still wasn't sure it was real.

As they turned the corner, Lydia pressed her hand to her stomach.

"I think I'm going to be sick."

Phillip turned to look at her and noted that she'd gone pale. "You don't have to go in there. You don't owe them anything."

"That's bullshit, and you know it. They are my family and they're worried about me. I disappeared, and that wasn't right. They deserve to be worried, and they deserve to be angry. I'm sorry they're going have the opportunity to ambush you if you go in with me."

"We're a team."

She reached for his hand and gave it a squeeze. "I like the sound of that."

Phillip parked his truck in front of the store and Lydia took a long, deep breath. "Okay, Let's go."

LYDIA HAD IMMEDIATELY SEEN that Pearl was working with a bride. There was some comfort there, at least she wouldn't make a scene. Phillip walked around the truck and took her hand, interlacing their fingers.

"Let's go," he said prompting her to move forward and walk through the front door.

Lydia pushed open the door and was met with the wide smile of Sunshine, who was standing behind the counter.

"Hey, Lydia," she chimed and then her smiled eased a bit. "Uncle Phillip, good morning to you." Her voice had a quizzical tone.

Phillip let the door close behind him and he gripped Lydia's hand tighter. "Morning, sweetheart. How are you today?"

"Good. I'm good." Her tone now told Lydia that she was the first to notice their hands, and it had thrown her into some uncertainty. "Lydia, Todd is in the office waiting for you," she said.

"Thanks." Lydia noticed they had caught Pearl's attention. She couldn't remember the last time she'd seen a scowl like that, and then her eyes, too, had gone wide. Her lips were pursed, but she quickly turned them into a smile as she gave her attention back to the bride she was working with.

Lydia went around the counter and opened the door to the office where Todd sat behind the desk. The moment he saw her, and Phillip, he rose to his feet. His face was red with anger, and because there was a customer in the store, he motioned her to enter with a curt nod.

Lydia walked through the door, Phillip still hand in hand with her as he'd promised.

"What in the hell are you doing?" he shot out in a heated whisper and then noticed their hands. "What in the hell is going on? Where have you been? Both of you?" He raked his fingers through his hair. "Sorry. You're adults. I'm confused. I'm mad. I'm confused," he said again, and that was when the door behind them flew open and Tyson Morgan burst into the room pushing Phillip up against the wall.

"Where in the hell have you been?" He had hold of Phillip's shirt and his arm had come up under his chin. "You don't get to take off with her and not tell us what's going on. What did you do?"

Lydia swiftly moved to her brother and pulled him back. "How dare you!"

"Dare *me*? I've spent the last fifteen years watching you run from this man, and now you're home and he disappears with you? Are you freaking kidding me? I know what went on fifteen years ago, and I know grandpa put a stop to it. So if you think I'm going to stand here and..."

Pearl swept into the room, slamming the door closed behind her.

"Would you all mind shutting up?" Her voice carried in tone, if not the volume. "I have a very particular bride out there who has just heard all of this and is in a bit of a panic. She has booked a venue with you, Lydia and Todd, and portraits with Jessie. She has Susan set up for catering and Audrey is doing her hair. We all have a lot at stake if you ruin this."

She narrowed her eyes on her husband who stood toe to toe with Lydia, and Phillip was pinned to the wall behind her.

"Back up," Pearl ordered her husband.

"You have no idea what he did," Tyson spoke through gritted teeth.

"Neither do you," she bit out the words. "Let Lydia be the one who shares that with us—if she wants to." Her eyes shifted to Lydia. "I'm going to see this bride out the door, and then I'll be back. No one leaves. And don't think you're not on my shit list. You are."

Pearl left the office and Tyson took a step backward. There was silence in the room, but Phillip rested his hands on Lydia's shoulders and she knew he was still on her side.

Todd sat behind the desk, and Tyson took a chair. Lydia and Phillip stood at the wall until Pearl returned a few minutes later with Audrey in tow.

With a calm that none of them had, Pearl closed the door.

"Now, like civilized adults, let's deal with what's going on," she began in her organizational tone she used when conducting meetings. "Lydia, you missed your meeting with Todd."

"I did."

"As soon as we're done here, you're having that meeting."

"Fine," Lydia snapped her answer.

"Phillip, you were asked to call me last night when you got her home safe and sound. You didn't call."

She felt him tense behind her. "You're right. I didn't call. I didn't take her home."

Lydia was sure everyone had already sensed that, but the air grew thicker with his admission. She saw her brother's hands fist, but he stayed seated where he was.

Phillip pulled her in closer. "I would have hoped you all knew how I've always felt about Lydia, and that I would take care of her no matter what. I have always worn my heart on my sleeve."

Pearl moved toward the center of the room with her calm

manner. "Okay. We've always known how you felt. But we've always known how Lydia felt, too." Lydia winced at that, but didn't interrupt. "Now, most of us, even those who are married to the family," she shifted a glance to her husband, "only assume that these feelings between the two of you were brought on from some affair gone bad. What we've never had was confirmation on that."

Lydia took a step toward her. "It started when I was seventeen. Phillip was twenty-one." She saw her brother's eyes widen and his face grew redder. "We kept it quiet because of the age difference. I hadn't even graduated, hell, I wasn't even old enough to vote, but I was in love. My grandfather found out about it before I turned eighteen, and he kept me under his thumb so that I wouldn't get any wild ideas. Now I understand why. He'd lost one daughter to a man—Tyson and Eric's mother—he wasn't going to lose a granddaughter."

"He was wrong to do that to you," Pearl defended her.

"Maybe, but you know how persuasive he is. You think your father is a bad seed—this is why our families were at odds. Both men could twist any fate in their direction at any cost."

Pearl moved closer to her. "So now that you're back from your year-long sabbatical, you're diving back in?"

Lydia reached for Phillip's hand. "Things happened that I never thought would happen to me—that I'd lose the love of my life, I'd be greatly successful, I'd be loved by my friends, and then I'd be kidnapped, raped, and that I'd kill a man." The words were raw, and she'd never said them like she had at that minute. Phillip's hand gripped hers tighter, and she noted the anger in her brother's eyes and the pity in Pearl's. "I took this past year to deal with all of that. That man took everything from me in a few hours. I took his life. That's not something you move on from. But you learn to deal with it." She spoke now through gritted teeth just as her brother had. "Part of my recovery was to deal with my past. I needed to know I could be touched by someone I trusted—someone I knew felt something deeper for me than physical attraction. Phillip is that someone. And I love him. I have always loved him."

The room was silent of even breath.

Pearl's eyes went wide as she stepped in front of her husband, no doubt to shield any attack he was willing to shell out as he stood from the chair.

"You love him?" she asked and looked at Phillip. "You love Phillip Smythe?" A smile crossed her lips and Lydia let out a grateful laugh.

"I do," she said as she turned to him. "I do love him."

He looked down into her eyes and pulled her into his arms. "And I love you. I have since the minute I met you."

The door opened again, and Bethany walked into the room, followed by Sunshine. Both sets of eyes went wide.

Bethany let out a laugh. "Okay, this is a sight. What did I miss?"

CHAPTER 25

*E*ventually the room had emptied out, Phillip had gone home, with the promise to come back for Lydia, and Todd had rescheduled their meeting for the next morning. Lydia sat alone in the office with her brother, who's eyes still were narrowed and his lips pursed.

"Let it out," she said from behind the desk. "You're pissed and you can hardly hold it in."

She'd been right. Tyson rose from his chair and paced the room. "For starters, don't ever say the word raped again." He batted back tears and wiped away the few that escaped. "I know what happened. I saw you come out of that goddamned house. The word—I can't deal with it, Lyd."

A year ago, that would be where she let loose on him and ripped him up one side and down another. But she'd learned to let that go and allow others to deal with her trauma in their way as well. She hadn't been the only one hurt by it. Her mother had said the same thing to her during a therapy session, and then started her own sessions to learn to deal with it.

"I'll never say it again."

He eased himself back down into a chair. "You're okay? I mean really okay?"

"I'm scared to death of my house. I'll never sleep there again, and Phillip promised me I'd never have to."

"So you'll sleep with him?"

The thought of the night before filled her mind and her heart, and she couldn't help but smile and nod. "If he'll have me."

"Can't imagine he'd ever turn you away."

Being very mindful of her brother's feelings, she still needed him to be her confidant. "He has someone else in his life. She was there the night before I was, but he says its nothing."

Tyson shook his head. "I've never known Phillip Smythe to not jump in fully to something—or someone. But I've never known him to lie either."

"I want to marry him."

Tyson's shoulders dropped. "What do you think Grandpa will say?"

"I don't give a damn. I haven't spoken to the man in over a year. He has no control over me anymore."

Tyson eased in to lean toward the desk and take her hands in his. "He sent you away."

"He did."

"He sent you away because of you and Phillip. Does Phillip know why?"

Lydia eased back in her seat. "Not yet, and it's not your place to bring it up. I'll tell him."

"Soon, Lyd. Soon."

Yeah, she agreed with a nod. Soon.

PHILLIP HAD WANTED to tinker in his garage, but he opted instead to park his truck in there so no one would know he was home.

He dug out a set of sheets he hadn't used on his bed in years, and threw out the ones he'd taken off after Parker had spent the night. Surely, Lydia would be sleeping in his bed that night.

A ball of guilt had solidified in his belly after leaving Lydia at the bridal store. She'd assured him she was fine, but he felt as if he should be there to protect her from her friends and her brother.

Then again, Lydia had never needed that.

Phillip finished making the bed and froze in place when he heard a vehicle pull up into his driveway. He managed a peek out the window and let out a breath when he noticed it was Todd Walker.

By the time Todd made it to the front door, Phillip had pulled it open.

"Todd."

"Let's talk," Todd said as he walked right past Phillip and into his house. "Got some beer? Whisky? A really strong pot of coffee brewed?"

Phillip looked at his watch. "It's noon."

"Question stands."

"Why don't I make us a pot of coffee, and what you do with the shot of whisky is up to you."

Todd followed him to the kitchen and sat at the table while Phillip made the coffee and poured them each a shot of whisky. Todd threw his back, while Phillip added his to his mug.

"What's got you all hot?" Phillip finally asked as he sat down across from Todd.

"First of all, don't hurt her. I don't think she's thinking this through all the way."

Okay, so he was there to defend Lydia's honor.

"I think she gave it a year's worth of thought. But I won't hurt her."

"You're right. I do think she gave it some thought." Todd

sipped his coffee and then pushed it away. "When she would call, she'd ask about you. She knew you'd be asking about her, that is. I was careful when I told her you'd been around here and there, or asked about her. I knew how she was with you."

"I've learned a lot this week. Lydia had made quite the case for hating me."

"Yeah, well, when I would tell her you asked about her, were concerned about her, or sent you best, she never got mad. I always assumed she'd have something negative to say. In fact, I think that hearing your name always made her feel better, but I didn't know what to think about that. I figured she was medicated or something."

That hadn't been something Phillip had considered. Was she medicated? Was this all going to fizzle out when she didn't have pharmaceutical support?

"Why are you telling me all of this?" he asked Todd.

"I suppose I'm trying to wrap my head around all of it. She's never missed a meeting. She's never shrugged off her responsibilities. And she's never given you the time of day."

"Everyone changes."

Todd nodded. "I wanted you to know how she reacted when I talked about you. Maybe all of this shouldn't have been such a surprise."

"Oh, it's a surprise," Phillip assured him. "I'm adjusting too. I think it was made to be a bigger deal than it was."

"True. I suppose if the *Bridal Mecca* were still standing, we wouldn't be quite this frantic. But that just added to the level of uncertainty in her life."

"I agree. Todd, I'll never hurt her. It doesn't mean she won't hurt, but I won't be behind it. And if I am, I'll stick it out until she's over it."

"Sorry I barged in here. Jessie didn't want me to say anything. She thought I should have just let it go."

"You care for her. I get it."

"I do." Todd stood. "I'm happy things are working out with you both."

"Thanks. Let everyone know it's all going to be okay."

CHAPTER 26

*L*ydia had called around six that night for him to pick her up from *The Garden Room* where she'd been finalizing plans with her mother.

When she walked out to his truck, her mother waved, and he returned the gesture.

"I should have come in to get you. It would make a better impression," he said as Lydia climbed into his truck.

"I wanted to be done with the day, and she saw me cracking."

He pulled away from the curb and took her hand. "She's okay with us?"

Lydia rested her head against the back of the seat and turned to look at him. "She's always known how I felt. In fact, she's always been on your side."

"I'm so charming, who wouldn't be?"

That made her laugh.

"I have dinner warming in the oven. I thought we'd get back to those steaks I made last night."

"It sounds like a perfect night."

THERE WAS a domestic bliss to having dinner on the table and doing dishes when it was finished. Could she easily fall into this rhythm?

Lydia was used to working all the time, but with the past year being all about her healing, she'd become more used to sitting quietly, breathing, and journaling. The full day of work, with everyone being tightly wound and protective, had worn her out.

The July night sang with the sounds of crickets and a warm breeze that rattled the trees. She and Phillip had opted to sit on his back-porch swing and just take in the peace.

Yes, she could get used to this domestic bliss.

"Did things settle down for you after I left this morning?" he asked running his fingers over her bare shoulders, as she'd opted for one of his tank tops when she'd returned home—to his home.

"Pearl had it out with me one more time. Todd scheduled for tomorrow, opting not to talk to me today. My brother had some deep words. Sunshine didn't know what to say, but she's very happy for you." He chuckled, and she continued. "My mother has always been on your side, as I said. Otherwise, it was a normal day."

"I get it. You've run in a different direction from me for years. This is going to take some time for everyone."

"I don't want it to. I've been working on this for a year. I feel like everyone should be up to my speed."

"Lydia, even *I'm* not up to your speed." He trailed his fingers up and down her arm. "Todd did stop by today."

"He's talking to you, huh?"

"Sort of. I think he was just wanting me to know that when he mentioned me over the past year, you didn't say anything bad."

"He noticed that, huh?"

"Was it intentional?"

She turned to look up into his eyes. "I'm not going to lie. The moment I saw you walk into that house, with that man's blood still on my hands, I knew I'd wasted fifteen years of my life being mad at you."

Phillip kissed the top of her head. "Did you hear about the townhouse yet?" he asked.

"She was still working on my offer. They didn't accept the first one."

"So you adjusted it?"

"Jean suggested I up it, just a little."

Phillip turned so they were face to face. "Why don't you retract your offer. Live here. Make this your home."

The words squeezed at her heart and she thought she might cry, because that was something she did now. "I'm not easy to live with. We've been at this a few days..."

"Plus fifteen years. Lydia, I've spent most of my life with you hating me. I know the not easy part of you."

She covered her mouth with her hand, and the tears began. This was what she wanted, but there was more she needed to tell him. She had to consider that this was all the bliss she could have with this man.

"When is your next day off?" she asked.

His eyes narrowed. "Friday, why?"

"Will you take me to Atlanta on Friday? I need to show you something."

A smile tugged at the corner of his mouth, and his eyes flashed between amused and annoyed. "What's in Atlanta?"

"I just have to show you something. Promise me you'll take me?"

"Of course I would."

"And can I stay here with you? Then after Friday we can decide how to let this play out."

Phillip raised his hand to her cheek and studied her. "I don't know if I want to wait until Friday. You're freaking me out right now."

Lydia lifted the hand he'd placed on her cheek, and pressed a kiss to his palm. "It'll wait."

Phillip pulled her back against him and moved the porch swing with his foot. The stars began to sparkle above them, and Lydia willed the tears back now. There was one more step in her recovery, and it would happen in Atlanta—where he might drive away and never speak to her again.

CHAPTER 27

They rose together and got ready for work together. When Phillip walked to the kitchen, his coffee mug was filled and ready to go.

"It always was hard to resist you in your uniform," Lydia moved to him and straightened his tie.

"You did a good job of it."

She laughed it off then pressed a kiss to his lips. "Do you still have time to take me by my house to get my car?"

"Yeah, no problem. What's on your schedule today?" He picked up his coffee and took a sip. He knew she used his maker and his grounds, but why did it taste so much better?

"I have my meeting with Todd. I have a meeting with a new bride who wants to see two venues. Then after lunch, Russell is going to meet me at my place and we're going to discuss fixing it up so I can rent it."

"Lydia Morgan, owner of the entire town."

"Income is nice, and I already own it."

"You're an impressive woman." He pulled her to him and kissed the top of her head. "But you promise me, you won't stay at the house alone. When you're done with Russell, you leave."

"I promise."

He pulled his keys from his pocket and took a gold one from the ring. "Here, this is yours now. Come and go as you like. You're safe here and welcome here. I want this to be your home when you're ready."

Lydia took the key and wrapped her hand around it. "How many of these are out there?"

"None. You'll be the first person to ever have a key to my house. I mean it, Lydia. You're the only one."

She bit down on her lip before rising on her toes to firmly plant a kiss on lips. "I love you."

"I love you, too."

Phillip waited for her to start her car and drive off toward town before he headed to the station. Never in all his life had he wished for a crime spree, but today he'd do anything to avoid going into the office.

Now he was going to have to face the music. Parker would be there. If she decided to play this up, she could have his badge. A decade of service to the town could be over before he even made it home.

It would be worth it, he thought as he pulled into the parking lot. If he had to give it all up for Lydia, he'd do it. Nothing had ever been more important than she was.

He was well aware of the risk factor in assuming everything was in order when it came to Lydia. A heated affair when she was a teenager and he was just cutting his teeth as an adult, didn't give them a solid foundation for a lifelong relationship. There was the fact that when things got too serious, Lydia would disappear too. It could happen again.

The more he thought about it, the more his mood soured. He was setting himself up for a fall.

As he stepped out of his truck, he heard his name called from the sidewalk. Ella Walker waved with a cheery smile. What were the chances she needed him to go with her and serve a client with something?

"Hey, Phillip. Nice to see you."

"Likewise. Headed into the station?"

Her lips puckered. "Have a client who needs a lawyer. Nothing big, but here I am."

"Happy Tuesday, huh?"

"How was your evening?" she asked, and he heard the humor in it, and he stopped walking.

"If you want the latest gossip, you'll have to ask her. I don't want to say something that she'll later take offense to."

Ella narrowed her eyes on him. "You're in a mood. I'm not looking for gossip. I'm rather happy with all the news I've been hearing the past few days. I love Lydia, and I don't want anything to take away her happiness. She damn well deserves to be happier than anyone else in this town."

Phillip placed a hand on Ella's shoulder. "You're right. I'm in a mood." He leaned in and kissed her cheek. "My evening was delightfully spent in the arms of a woman I've loved my entire life, under the stars on my porch swing."

Ella smiled. "That sounds like a lovely night."

Together they walked into the building and parted ways as Ella checked in and was taken to see her client and Phillip walked to his office.

The squad room appeared to be quiet. Those who were at their desks were busy filing papers, others, he had to assume, were out keeping the streets safe.

Without turning his head, he saw that Parker wasn't at her desk, and he let out a breath of relief.

Phillip walked through the door to his office and noted that all the blinds had been closed on the windows. From behind him, he heard his door close and the lock engage.

When he turned, Parker leapt at him. Her legs came around

his waist, her arms around his neck, and her mouth planted firmly on his as he stumbled toward the door to hold himself up, dropping his hat to the floor.

Her mouth moved from his and trailed kisses down his neck, as he caught his breath.

"You know, you taking a personal day at the beginning of the week isn't like you." Her mouth clamped back down on his. "Where ya been, Smythe?"

When she advanced again to kiss him, he turned his head and pried her from his waist.

"You should come with a warning label," he said as she found her balance on her feet.

"You're mad," she assessed as she studied his face. "We're not okay here, are we?"

Phillip rubbed the back of his hand over his lips and unlocked the office door. Hopefully, no one on the other side heard anything. He picked up his hat, hung it on the hook, and walked around the side of his desk.

"We need to talk."

Her eyes went wide as if she knew what he might tell her.

Moving toward his desk, Parker eased herself into one of the chairs. "Someone found out about us, didn't they? Shit. I'm going to lose my job."

"No, no," he offered as he sat behind his desk. "I don't think anyone knows anything. Dear God, I hope not."

She looked offended, but he knew that wasn't the case in this situation.

"Then what's up? You never called me after I left your place. You didn't come by last night. I thought we had something good here."

No, he thought, they'd had something temporary all along, and it only filled each of their needs for physical companionship. But that's all it meant.

"Parker, I think we shouldn't see each other anymore."

Her eyes went wide, but then quickly narrowed on him. "You do? You get to make the decision alone?"

"Usually when people break up, one person instigates it. I'm called out on cases like that at least once a week."

"And what happened between the time I woke up in your bed until now? What did I do?"

He found it easier to stand and have the conversation, that way he could pace. "You didn't do anything. This is all on me."

"You don't like me? I'm okay to have sex with, but that's it?"

He'd assumed that was the plan all along, but had she been more invested?

"Listen, things change, and right now I need to tend to the changes going on in my life."

Parker pressed her fingers to her eyes. "This is about that woman, isn't it? That woman who was kidnapped last year and killed that guy." She looked up at him searching for answers. "She's back, and now I'm not important."

"I didn't say you weren't important."

"You said we shouldn't see each other anymore. That means I'm not important, because for the past few months I've been extremely important to you."

She had been. She'd kept his mind off of Lydia, and that wasn't fair to Parker at all. "I don't know what else I can say. I'm sorry."

"Well, so am I. I thought you were a bit more upstanding than this, Phillip Smythe. And to think I risked my job for you." She pushed back in the chair and stood, adjusting the items on her belt. "What a waste of time."

Parker pulled open his office door and Ella stood just beyond it looking his way. Perhaps what had happened had been heard after all.

CHAPTER 28

*T*odd pushed contracts around the desk, plugged in the alcohol order, and blew out more breaths in an hour than Lydia had all year in therapy. Finally she'd had enough of the silent treatment and she dropped a stack of contracts on the floor.

Todd's head came up and he turned to her. "What did you do that for?"

"It got you talking." She admitted, kicking her feet up on the desk. "Are you seriously going to ignore me all week? I overslept one meeting—first time in my life, too."

He blew out one more breath and knelt down to pick up the contracts, so she joined him on the floor.

"Todd, what's wrong?"

He sat back on his heels. "This isn't how it was supposed to be when you got home. We weren't supposed to be rebuilding everything from the ground up. By now I figured you'd have kicked me to the curb, but I'm still here, and I want to be. Everything is twice its size now, and when the *Bridal Mecca* is rebuilt, you'll have more area to cover."

"So where is our problem?"

"You're going to get hurt," he said matter-of-factly. "You've fought Phillip as long as I've known you. He hasn't even come around the past two months, and now you're sleeping with him. You don't need any more heartache."

Lydia sat back on the floor and stared at Todd. Did they all feel this way? Usually this was exactly how she would approach things, but it didn't feel that way to her when it came to Phillip.

"I'm going to be okay, Todd. No matter what, I'm going to be okay."

"I know you will be. He came in all the time asking about you. He genuinely cares about you."

She smiled as she picked up one of the contracts. "He loves me."

"I think he just might."

THEY SEEMED to be fine to get some work done the rest of the day, and even discuss what jobs Todd would oversee going forward. He had decided that being part of the bridal business was where he wanted to be, especially with his fiancée having one of the stores in the *Bridal Mecca*.

It was just shy of five o'clock when Lydia finalized the last contract from the meeting she'd had with a bride that morning. She closed up her folders and turned off the computer. Sunshine peeked her head into the office.

"I'm heading out. Pearl is finishing with a bride. I'll walk out with you."

Lydia studied the younger woman, Phillip's niece. "My car is just out front. I'll be okay. And you can text your uncle and let him know too."

Sunshine laughed. "I'm not very good at that, am I?"

Lydia laughed. "I've gotten everyone else's opinion on me and Phillip. What's yours?"

Sunshine smiled sweetly. "He deserves to have someone love him. He gets a bad rap for being the guy who's in on everything in town, but really, he's a good guy."

"I couldn't agree more. I won't treat him like I did in the past. I promise."

Sunshine's smile grew and lifted to her eyes. "I believe you. I'll see you tomorrow."

Lydia packed up her things and put them into the bag she carried with her. As she shut the door to the office, Pearl excused herself from her bride and walked toward her.

"Heading out?" she asked.

"I am. We have that meeting with the contractor tomorrow, so I'm going to go home and look over the items we want to discuss with them."

"I'll be ready. Where are you going for the night?"

Lydia reached for Pearl's hand and gave it a squeeze. "Until further notice, I'll be staying with Phillip. He's asked me to move in with him."

Pearl let out a laugh as she folded Lydia into her arms. "This is so strange. I'm so happy for you, but you have to understand—so strange."

Lydia laughed. "I know, but, Pearl, I'm happy."

Pearl stepped back and looked her over. "You look happy. Okay, go home. I'll see you in the morning."

Pearl went back to her bride and Lydia left the store walking directly to her car.

"Lydia Morgan?"

She turned when she heard her name called.

Walking toward her was a woman police officer in uniform, her blonde hair pulled back in a ponytail.

"Can I help you?" she asked, wondering if Pearl saw the woman approach her.

"I just needed to see you for myself."

Lydia's mouth had gone dry, and she gripped the keys in her fingers in case the woman came at her.

"See what? Did I do something wrong?"

The woman stopped at the back of Lydia's car. Her hands rested on her belt, and Lydia noticed that she wasn't carrying her gun.

"You have no idea who I am, do you?"

Lydia shook her head. "I'm sorry. I don't."

"He didn't even tell you about me, did he?"

It was becoming clearer now and Lydia bit down on her lip as she felt it begin to tremble. "I assume you're talking about Phillip."

"Of course I'm talking about Phillip. Now do you know who I am?"

"You know my name, but I don't know your name."

The woman laughed. "Did he tell you he broke things off with me this morning? I've been with him for months, and now suddenly he's with you."

Lydia noticed the name on the officer's badge. "Officer Davis, I don't know you. I'm sorry if things didn't work out with you and Phillip. He told me he'd been seeing someone."

"He told you I slept in his bed just a few days ago?"

Lydia swallowed hard. "I'm aware of that. And nothing happened with us before that." None of this sounded good on her part. God, she shouldn't have pushed him into having sex with her as part of her therapy. There was plenty of time for them to move forward. Looking at the woman standing before her, and thinking of the anger that had surrounded everyone she loved that morning, she realized she might have moved too fast.

"Well, I guess that makes it better." The woman pursed her lips. "I could have his job for this."

"I suppose you could. But what would happen to your job?" Lydia asked.

The woman winced. "Be warned. I don't see him settling

down, so you'll be in the same boat soon. He's not built for long term relationships that are out in the open."

That was all the woman had to say, because she turned back to her car and drove away. Lydia let out a breath and the tears poured down her cheeks.

CHAPTER 29

They hadn't told each other what time they would get home from work. One thing Phillip knew about Lydia was that she worked all the time. Between all of her businesses, it would be hard to tie her down to a regular schedule. He didn't have much of a set schedule either. Crime happened all the time. Often, he was pulled from bed to serve the people. Though, he never minded.

He'd stopped by the flower store, where Bethany had arranged a beautiful bouquet for him to take home to Lydia.

He rather enjoyed the thought of going home to someone—to Lydia.

Phillip parked in front of his house and a warmth flooded him when he saw Lydia's car parked in the driveway. This was a new start—the way it should have always been.

He gathered his things and headed into the house. When he didn't see her right away, he went straight to his home office and locked away his gun. Fresh on his mind was the way she'd reacted when he'd worn it to her house.

As he walked through the kitchen, he noticed her on the

porch swing. To her right was a bottle of wine and a box of tissue.

He picked up the bouquet and walked out onto the porch. Her eyes went directly to his belt, assumedly checking for his gun, and then rose to meet his. She'd been crying. This he wasn't prepared for.

"Sweetheart, what's wrong?" He discarded the flowers onto another chair and sat down next to her. "Why the tears?"

"You said it wasn't important. That you didn't love her. It was only physical."

Phillip narrowed his gaze on her. "What are we talking about?"

"Officer Davis."

An ache formed in his chest and he had to use the palm of his hand against his breastbone to ease the away the pain.

"Why are we talking about Parker?"

"Oh good. She has a first name," Lydia snipped as she wiped away the fresh tears.

"I didn't love her."

"Yeah, but I don't think that's how she felt about you."

Phillip ran his fingers over his chin. "You talked to her?"

"Sure did." Lydia looked at her full glass of wine, but never sipped. "She met me outside of Pearl's store. She seemed to be doing me a service, letting me know you're not a serious relationship guy and I'd get hurt. I think she really just wanted to see me—get a feel of what replaced her overnight."

The ache was back, but this time he let it hurt. Parker had been replaced overnight—literally. He hadn't liked how any of it went down. He'd struggled with it all day, but he'd give up anything to have Lydia. That had always been the case.

"She shouldn't have done that."

"No. She shouldn't have. But then again, I shouldn't have come to you looking for you to fix me when I knew there was someone else. I dismissed her entirely as if she wasn't important."

"Lydia, you're very important to me. I can't imagine there would have been anyone in the world I wouldn't have sent away just to have you tell me you love me."

She let out a hard laugh. "Makes me out to be some kind of home wrecker, doesn't it?"

"Parker will get over it."

"What if she doesn't? What if she uses it against you, and then everything you've worked so hard for is destroyed? Is that worth it?"

"Absolutely," he said without even thinking about it.

Phillip moved to his knees and knelt in front of Lydia, demanding her attention by taking her glass of wine and setting it on the ground.

"What we had once upon a time fueled us to get to here. This is all new though. We're adults now. We make the calls. We make all the decisions. I would never have married Parker. In fact, I was getting a bit disturbed that she'd just show up. But yes, it was all physical, and I needed that. I thought that was what she needed, too. I'm sorry for what I did to her if it wasn't mutual." And the ache in his chest deepened. "But since I was a young man, it's always been you. I thought never in my life would you come to me or say the things you've said to me, but it was still always you. Having you gone this past year was like reliving that year you disappeared all over again. And knowing you would refuse me when you returned, well that was probably what led me to looking for comfort. I'm not ashamed, but I'm sad that I hurt someone. And I'm bothered that she hurt you with her words."

Lydia blinked away the fresh tears. "I didn't mean to disrupt anyone's life by trying to put mine back on track."

"Of course you didn't. That's not how you work."

A smile tugged at the corner of her mouth. "I'll hire you if you get fired."

Phillip chuckled as he pulled her to him. "It would be worth it to get fired then."

"I love you. I didn't mean to bring you drama."

Phillip pushed her hair from her forehead. "Again, it was worth it. You're in my house, and this is where I hope you want to stay."

"I think it is. I got the townhouse, but I'm going to lease it out."

Now he laughed. "Lydia Morgan, the real estate queen of Georgia."

"I think I'll put that on my business cards." She looked past him. "Are those flowers for me?"

"Yes, I thought they'd be a nice gesture for my new roommate."

"They're lovely."

"I also made sure I wasn't on call for Friday. We can head to Atlanta any time you want."

He saw the flash of dread in her eyes, but it was quickly replaced with a gracious smile. "We should leave in the morning. I'll be ready to go early."

CHAPTER 30

*H*ighly sensitive to the feelings of those around her, regarding her love life, her living situation, and her attention to her businesses, Lydia put in extra effort to get back on track.

She was prompt to her meetings, and sent out extra emails to verify details. She'd taken Pearl to the hotel for high tea, and hired Russell to update her house. Taking as much as she could from Todd's list of things he needed to tend to, she suggested he and Jessie take a few days off to do wedding planning. That was met with a scowl, because he was over planning weddings, but he was appreciative for the time to dote on Jessie.

Things would go back to normal, she thought as she sat at her desk looking at spreadsheets.

They'd had their meeting with the contractors who were rebuilding the *Bridal Mecca* and they'd made plans for that second story to the building. It would be well past spring before the building was ready, but she was okay with that. Everyone had relocated their businesses, and no one seemed to be hurting. Business had thrived, and she credited them all for having built a solid reputation that could withstand such a blow.

She'd come into a few new properties as well, and her mother rather enjoyed working with her at *The Garden Room* again.

But dread for Friday filled her heart, and she wondered if her life would take another hit after they returned. What she had to do in Atlanta would be the final stages of her healing—from everything. Her kidnapping and sexual assault, she took that in stride. There were nightmares, and she looked over her shoulder everywhere she went. She locked her doors, and relocked them just to be safe. But she understood that. She'd killed a man—but he had killed first. There had been many sessions on how she felt taking a life, but in the end, she had stopped him. Then there were the sessions, the many, many sessions, on her grandfather uprooting her life right before she'd turned eighteen. He'd sent her away *for her own good.* He'd made sure she had no contact with anyone at home, especially Phillip. There were threats, and bribes, and in the end she stayed away longer than she'd needed to, but she didn't seek help then. And now she knew she should have. What her grandfather had stolen from her was a chance to have the life she had wanted.

Things worked out for her grandfather, he'd said that to her face and she'd locked herself in her room for nearly a week. Even as a grown woman who had spent hours in therapy discussing her grandfather, she still couldn't believe that was what he'd said to her. He had no idea the damage he'd done to her.

But she'd let him control her for years after. She'd taken his bribes and his money to start her empire. Not many women owned property before they were twenty-one, but Lydia Morgan had. She owned stock in their ranch, in small business startups, and real estate. By the time she was twenty-five, she'd made her first million dollars, and she'd tucked it away so her grandfather would never know what she'd done on her own. No one knew her worth but her. There was no need to flaunt it. She'd just continue to grow that empire, and she'd do it to honor what she lost, not to spite it.

Perhaps she'd been moved to be successful so that she'd stayed busy and Phillip Smythe wouldn't play havoc with her mind. She'd been in and out of relationships, much like Phillip and Parker's. They hadn't meant anything. They were just physical. If someone became attached, she fled.

She'd been told in therapy, that was her coping mechanism to never having the love she craved be taken from her again.

Phillip never deserved the way she treated him. She'd come back hateful, and instead of turning that hate toward her grandfather who had sent her away, she turned it toward Phillip, which earned her praise from her grandfather.

One breath.

Two breaths.

Three breaths, and she calmed herself back down enough to continue working on the spreadsheets. It was a new starting point. The past was the past, and the present was a present. She'd been given another chance, and she was happy. Phillip loved her, and she loved him. She always had loved him. They could overcome anything—together.

PHILLIP SAT at his desk processing reports when Ella tapped on his door.

He'd expected to see her. He invited her in, and she closed the door behind her.

"To what do I owe the pleasure?" he asked as she took the seat in front of his desk.

"About six of us saw what went on in here yesterday and heard it too. Not all the blinds were closed," she admitted. "Listen, choose one, but don't let Lydia be led on if you're not serious about her. And yes, this comes from the woman married to the man Lydia made a play for."

Phillip winced at that. They'd both been desperate for affection, and Lydia had thrown hers at Gerald once or twice.

"I guess the part that wasn't heard was me telling her we were done. There's nothing there, Ella. I promise you."

"I know what Lydia means to you, and I don't think you would hurt her on purpose. But I'm with everyone else, it's a little strange that after all these years of avoiding you, now she's with you. Does that make sense?"

"More than you can possibly imagine. I've waited for her to come around for years, mostly giving up on it. She trusts me, and that means the world to me. I would never hurt her on purpose."

"So what happens now? You work with that lady."

Phillip shrugged. "I haven't seen her today, and when I do, we will have words. She went to Lydia, and that was unacceptable."

"Did she start something with her?"

"I think she was just discouraging. But that isn't going to fly with me. I know my job is on the line, and I knew that going in. She's not worth it, but Lydia is."

Ella offered him a smile, and then stood. "I have your back if you ever need it, Phillip. I have seen what you do in this town, and it would be a shame if you lost your job over something like this."

"I appreciate that."

CHAPTER 31

*I*t wasn't long after Ella left his office that the commissioner came in and closed the door. He sat down in front of Phillip's desk, crossing his legs at the ankle and resting his folded hands on his stomach.

"It appears that Parker Davis has requested a transfer to a different station. Do you know anything about that?"

There was a bit of relief, and Phillip felt it in his chest. "She didn't discuss that with me."

The commissioner raised his eyebrows. "I had a few officers tell me you had an argument with her yesterday."

It was better that they had told him that, than what had happened when he had walked into the room. "I suppose we did."

"Want to let me in on what it was about?"

"Would rather not."

Captain nodded slowly. "I also heard she paid a visit to Lydia Morgan, the woman who was kidnapped last year and killed that man."

"I had heard the same."

"I don't have a problem if she did so, while in uniform, stating

153

police business. But from what I understand, it was a personal visit, and perhaps meant to be intimidating."

"I understand that that might have been her motive. However, I don't think she caused any harm."

"I think we can be safe, in assuming that we understand each other, that when it comes to Officer Davis, you and she should probably not have any further communication."

So, he was being let off the hook. For that, he could be grateful.

"Understood."

The commissioner stood up. "Aside from the change in personnel, is everything else going okay for you?"

"Couldn't be better actually."

"Good. I'm glad to see you've been taking a few days off too. You deserve it. You've worked harder than any other person in this department. You let me know if you need anything."

"Will do."

THEY QUICKLY HAD FALLEN into a routine, and Phillip found great comfort in it. He was as skeptical as the rest of them, and he hated to be that way. He'd gotten quite used to Lydia blowing him off and avoiding him altogether. But he had to admit, having her in his arms every night, and hearing the words *I love you*, he would never tire of that.

Thursday night he watched as Lydia moved about the house, cleaning, organizing, and avoiding conversation. He didn't push the issue. He knew that whatever waited for him in Atlanta was making her nervous.

He had tried not to think about it, the wondering what she wanted to see. Maybe it was a business venture. Maybe it was something from her past. Maybe there was a store with a fantastic dress, and she just wanted to see it for herself.

After they had gone to bed, he'd heard her get back up and move about the house. By the time he woke up, she was already showered, ready, and sitting at the kitchen table with a cup of coffee.

"It looks like you're ready to go," he said pouring himself a cup of coffee.

"I love you, Phillip. Don't ever forget, that no matter how I treated you, I have always loved you."

Her voice wobbled a bit, and he turned to see her eyes red with tears.

"We don't have to go to Atlanta. I don't want to go anywhere that's going to upset you."

"No, we have to go. I have to face this part of my past in order to move on."

"You realize this scares me? I have no idea what awaits us in Atlanta."

"It scares me too, but I can't go forward without you being there with me."

Phillip pulled her from her chair and wrapped his arms around her tight. "No matter what, I will be there for you. You can count on me."

Lydia looked up into his eyes. "I'm counting on that."

CHAPTER 32

There was more traffic than Lydia had thought there would be for a Friday morning. It was slowing down their drive, and she simply wanted to get their trip to Atlanta over with.

Most of her adult life, she'd avoided Atlanta. There just weren't any good memories there. Why would she ever want to challenge her emotions by going socially?

The closer they got to the city, the more nauseated she became. Phillip had taken her hand. "You do realize I'm on auto pilot. I have no idea where I'm going."

"There is a park I want to take you to." She gave him directions and sat back as he navigated the streets of Atlanta until he came to park along the edge of the grassy area.

"Okay," he said putting his truck in park. "We're here."

Lydia sat still in her seat, her eyes averted to her clasped hands in her lap. It had been fifteen years since she'd been there. Fifteen years ago she was just shy of eighteen and old enough to do what she'd wanted. She'd been held back by her grandfather's sheer power and his money.

"Why don't we just go home, Lydia. I don't know what it is you want to share with me, but you're freaking me out."

Lydia turned to Phillip.

One breath.

Two breaths.

Three breaths.

"Here's the deal. After today, you'll never want to speak to me again. After today, I'll be a part of your past you wish you'd have just left behind. After today, you won't love me anymore."

His eyes were wide and he rubbed his hand over his mouth. "I'm turning this truck around and we're going home." He reached for the ignition, and Lydia pulled back his hand.

"Even though you'll hate me, will you please see that I get home and take me to my brother's? From there, I'll figure everything else out."

She opened the door and stepped out onto the sidewalk, Phillip quickly following behind. He took her hand, and she found comfort in the fact that he was dismissing what she'd just told him. But it wouldn't be long.

"What is this park?" he asked, moving her along to tell her story.

The lake before them buzzed with people biking and walking. Children played on the playground, and the sound of the breeze in the trees forced her to close her eyes and continue to take deep breaths.

"This is where my grandfather sent me all those years ago," she began. "To Atlanta. Away from you."

"You were this close?"

"I was." She continued to walk the grassy knoll of the park, Phillip's hand in hers. "He put me up in a boarding house if you will. It was for runaway teens that they wouldn't send back home, but they didn't want to get away. Privately funded, so it wasn't as if they could shut it down."

"He locked you away."

"I was cared for," she assured him as they continued to walk the path that narrowed toward a lane of trees. "I finished my schooling privately and graduated early—also privately. You had gotten on with the police force. I remember getting a letter from Tyson that told me he'd seen you giving a speeding ticket," she said as she chuckled and Phillip drew her closer to him as they walked down the wooded path that led toward a gateway.

"Lydia, he kidnapped you. He should have been locked up for that."

"He sent me to a very secure boarding school," she offered as they crossed under the arch of the gateway. It was then they stopped and Phillip looked around them. They'd crossed into a cemetery, shadowed by trees.

She continued to walk with his hand in hers. "You see, in his eyes, and the eyes of many in the community, I was much too young to be with a man of twenty-one."

"You don't have to tell me that twice. My mother still reminds me of that, even when she asks about your well-being."

"Your mother is a wonderful lady."

"She adores you," he added.

"Anyway, it wasn't that he didn't trust my love, it was his reputation in business that would be marred."

Phillip slowed his walk until they stopped. "He sent you away so you wouldn't embarrass him by dating me?"

Lydia walked again, this time taking one of the paths that led to an area crowded with headstones. She saw Phillip's eyes widen when he saw the dates on the headstones. Some only had one day, others a few weeks or a few years.

"Phillip, I was pregnant when he sent me away. That's why he sent me away." That was when the dam broke and her tears spilled down her cheeks. "I was pregnant with our child."

His eyes were wide and the color drained from his face. "Lydia..."

"I'm sorry I've never told you."

. . .

PHILLIP FELT his knees go weak. He wasn't so sure he wasn't having a heart attack. Pressing his hand to his chest, he knelt down on the hard ground between the headstones and tried to catch his breath.

A baby.

Lydia knelt down in front of him, her cheeks streaked with the tears that continued to fall. He thought about her not wanting him to see her body when they'd made love, and then that stipulation eased. Now he thought of the tiny scars that softened her stomach—the kind of scars made when a woman carries a baby. His baby. Their baby. He was a father.

He sucked in air, but the thickness of the Atlanta air made it hard to catch his breath.

"I have a baby? We have a baby? I'm a father?" The questions shot out of him.

"Her name was Emma Grace."

"You named her after grandmothers."

"I did."

He sucked in more air, his head spinning until he thought he'd pass out right there on the path. And then it hit him. "You said her name was. You gave her up for adoption?" He realized where he was sitting, and that nausea was pushing through.

Lydia stood and walked through the headstones. Then she dropped herself in front of one of them and he could hear the sobs echo among the trees.

It took a moment to assess his legs. Could he stand? Would he have to crawl?

He managed to his feet. Walking toward Lydia, he saw her body convulse with the sound of her sobs. It was then that he saw the headstone she'd fallen in front of.

EMMA GRACE MORGAN-SMYTHE

OCTOBER 10 - OCTOBER 15

The tears choked him and he, too, fell to the ground next to her. His daughter lay in a grave in a park in Atlanta, and he'd never known about her. Lydia's grandfather had robbed him of knowing about Emma. He'd taken Lydia away from him. She'd had to endure this alone.

Phillip wrapped an arm around her and pulled her to him.

"What happened to her?" he asked, but he didn't even recognize his own voice.

"Her heart hadn't developed correctly," she said through her sobs. "She looked just like you," she managed before she collapsed against him.

As she sobbed against his chest, Phillip linked their fingers, and his attention was drawn to the tattoo on her wrist.

He moved her arm to look at it closer. "This is for her, right?"

Lydia lifted tear-filled eyes to meet his. "Yes. I wasn't here to visit her, and this was one way to be near her. Her heart is mine —for eternity."

Phillip kissed the top of her head and held her as they grieved together over their daughter's grave. Fifteen years of sadness squeezed at his heart.

And then the anger pushed through.

Fifteen years Emma Grace lay in that grave. Fifteen years and Lydia had never mentioned that she'd had his child.

CHAPTER 33

They sat at her grave sobbing for over an hour. Lydia no longer cared about the pain of what she'd gone through fifteen years ago, or the trauma she'd lived through since. She'd seen the moment his eyes had gone from sad to angry.

His arms had held her until they both figured they could walk back to the truck and manage their way home.

The ride back was silent. She wasn't sure what she would say, or if she could come up with words at all. What was he thinking? It was a lot to take in.

When they returned to town, he'd done as she'd asked and dropped her off at Pearl and Tyson's house, driving away before they'd even opened the door, which proved to her that he was done with her.

She'd broken his heart, and she deserved a lifetime of his silence now. At least she'd had the past few weeks.

Pearl opened the door and swiftly moved to her as her knees went weak.

"Lydia, what happened? What's wrong?" Her arms had come around her.

"I took him to Emma," she sobbed.

"Emma. Who is Emma?" she asked as she helped Lydia into the house.

Tyson moved to them and scooped up his sister as she cried into his shoulder. His eyes shifted to Pearl.

"What did he do to her?"

Pearl shrugged. "She said she took him to see Emma."

Tyson let out a long breath and kissed his sister's forehead before carrying her to the sofa and laying her down.

"He didn't take that well?" Tyson asked Lydia as he brushed her hair from her forehead.

"I should have told him. I should have spent the past fifteen years mourning with him, not being angry at him that she ever existed."

Pearl stood beyond Tyson looking down at them. "Who is Emma?"

Tyson waited for Lydia to given him a nod and the turned to reach for Pearl's hand.

"Emma was Lydia and Phillip's daughter."

Pearl's other hand moved to her chest and she then too fell to her knees. "Lydia, I had no idea."

"No one did but Tyson and my grandfather. I wasn't quite eighteen."

"Sweetheart, you never should have had to bear this alone." She exchanged looks with Tyson, and Lydia knew he'd have the wrath of Pearl to deal with later for never telling her. But he'd kept her secret as she'd always asked him to do. "I'm going to get you some tea," Pearl said before disappearing into the kitchen.

"I've lost them both, all over again," Lydia said as she wiped the tears that continued to flow. "This is what I've worked so hard for, to be right here, alone again."

"Bullshit. Give him time. He needs to process this."

"He's so angry, Tyson."

"He should be. Grandpa never should have taken you away. I should have fought for you. I could have been your guardian." He scrubbed his hand over his face as if it was something he'd thought about over the years. "But I was embarrassed too, I have to admit, and it had nothing to do with me."

"You have to talk to him—to Phillip. You have to tell him what I went through. You have to..."

She couldn't come up with the words to finish. She'd spent fifteen years punishing the man for her secret. She'd lost their daughter and now she'd lost him. Her heart would never mend, and she wasn't sure she had the right tools to cope with this loss.

PHILLIP DROVE THE DIRT ROAD, nearly an hour out of town, toward the big house he'd been to many times. It was time to confront the man who had single-handedly ruined his life.

He couldn't care that there was a time when the love between him and Lydia was frowned upon. It was as real then as it was now. There was no way in hell he was going to go another day without telling the man what he thought about what he'd done— especially now that he knew what had happened.

Phillip sped down the road to the house and into the circle in front of the door. As soon as he stepped out of his truck, the front door opened.

A fragile old man stood there, his hands on a walker. Her grandfather hadn't aged well, he thought, but it wasn't going to hold him back from telling him what he thought.

"Officer Smythe, I didn't call for police assistance. You're trespassing," his voice shook as he spoke.

"I am trespassing, and if you want police assistance you'd better call for it now. I have some words for you, and I'm angry as hell."

The man narrowed his eyes on him. "You always did think you could do whatever you wanted. You caused my poor Lydia a lot of pain."

"Oh, not me. She was perfectly happy until you stepped in."

"She was young."

"She sure was, but that isn't the point. You locked her away. You took her from her home and locked her up."

"She'd disgraced me."

"She was having my baby." His voice rang out.

The old man lifted his chin. "And what a disgrace that was."

Phillip balled his fists to his side. "The baby died."

"Grateful that the Lord knew better than to let it live. You'd never be in the position you're in now had it lived and had Lydia had anything to do with you. She's a very successful woman now, and that's no thanks to you."

Phillip moved toward him, but the man stood in the doorway unphased.

"There is no grace in knowing my daughter died. *My* daughter. You had no right to do to her what you did. I should have been there for her. I should have known about the baby. I should have been there when she died." His voice rose in pitch and volume. "I'm going to marry her, and we will have more babies. She will still be successful, and we'll be together. You cannot keep her from loving me."

"She will make her own decision. She's chosen to live her life without me," he said, and Phillip heard the tug of regret in his voice. "If she makes one wrong move, she could lose everything, and having a baby might just do that to her. My daughter had a baby, and I lost her too."

And there it had been, the truth to all the sadness in the old man's heart. His daughter had chosen Everett Walker over him, and from then on, any woman choosing a man over him should suffer.

"I feel sorry for you. You'll die alone out here. Love is a strong emotion. It can, and it will carry her through. I swear it. I love Lydia, sir. And from here on out, I will spend my life taking care of her."

With that, Phillip walked back to his truck and sped off down the road.

CHAPTER 34

The drive back to Atlanta was quiet. Phillip's mind filled with a million thoughts, all of them from moments scattered over the past fifteen years. He had focused on his career when she disappeared and continued to do so as Lydia suffered in peace.

His heart squeezed in his chest, and again nausea swirled in his stomach. Damn her grandfather for being a dictator. It was no wonder his own daughter had fled his control.

Phillip stopped by the store and picked up a bouquet of flowers to put on his daughter's grave. Then he drove to the cemetery he'd visited that morning.

She deserved flowers on that grave every day. He'd have made sure there were flowers there every day had he known. Tears stung his eyes again, as they had hours earlier. The love he felt for the child he didn't even know both warmed and crushed him.

He sat down in front of her headstone and placed the flowers on the ground.

"Emma, I'm your daddy," he said as the tears fell from his eyes and shook his voice. "I love you, and I always will. Your mama loves you too. She never would have left you here had I known about you. You should be where we are," he said as if he were deciding how he was going to handle this from here on. "I'm going to make sure you're with us, where you belong, sweet baby. I love your mama. I'm going to marry your mama and give you brothers and sisters. And I'll make sure you have flowers every day. You watch over us, and keep us safe, sweet baby."

Phillip traced her beautiful name with his fingers, honored that his mother's name was there as well as his last name. Even in death and trauma, Lydia hadn't forgotten him.

As soon as he could see clearly, he rose and headed to the office that was near the road. It was time to find out how they could move his baby back home.

MONDAY MORNING, Phillip parked outside of *Pearl's Bridal Boutique* and turned off the engine to his truck. His dress shoes shone, and he brushed the wrinkles from his black pants.

He straightened his tie and slid on the jacket to finish off the suit. As he pulled the bouquet of flowers from his passenger seat, the front door of the store opened and Pearl flew toward him.

"Where in the hell have you been? Do you know what you're putting her through? Do you know how beside herself she is? You had no right..." she stopped as she looked at him. "What are you doing?"

"Is she here? I'd like to speak to her," he said.

"Phillip, she's fragile. What are you doing?"

Phillip took Pearl's hand and moved her from the sight of the window. "I'm hurting too. I would never, ever have let her do that by herself. My daughter was taken from me and kept a secret. She should have been celebrated."

"So you're what, you're going to win her over with flowers? She did what she thought was right."

"And you're doing what you think is right by standing in my way. You know how I feel about her. I would never—ever hurt her."

Pearl batted back tears. "You still love her?"

"She's the only woman I've ever loved. We need to deal with what happened, but I love her."

Pearl pressed her manicured fingers to her lips. "She's in the office. She's in a dark place."

"I understand."

Phillip turned back to the store and walked inside. His niece smiled and greeted him, and he smiled back, but he kept moving.

Without knocking, he pushed open the office door. Todd stood from his chair, and Lydia lifted her head. She must have spent the past two days crying, because he hardly recognized her.

Todd looked at him, then looked him over. He'd opened his mouth as if he'd had something to say, but he never said anything.

Lydia stood from behind the desk. "What are you doing here? What are you wearing?" she asked as if both things were equally as strange to her.

"I need you to come with me."

"I'm working," her words began to tremble.

"Todd will take over. I need you."

Todd moved toward the door where Pearl and Sunshine stood.

Lydia walked around the desk toward Phillip. "Why are you all dressed up? Where have you been? God, are you speaking to me?"

She covered her mouth with her hands as if to keep herself quiet.

Phillip handed her the flowers. "These are for you. Emma has a matching set."

Now the tears fell from her eyes. He reached his hand to her cheek and brushed them away.

"It'll take six weeks, but I want to have a funeral for Emma."

"A funeral."

"I've arranged to have her brought here, so she's laid to rest where we can be near her."

Lydia set the flowers on the desk and leaned up against it. Phillip moved closer in case she collapsed. He knew he was dropping a lot of information on her.

"She'll be here?"

"In the center of town. I have the plot. It's under a beautiful tree."

"Phillip..."

"I promised her sisters and brothers. I asked her to watch over us, and I would also make sure she had flowers every day."

Lydia's eyes were wide, but she didn't speak. He was sure she couldn't if she tried.

He'd seen Jessie and Audrey join the others at the door from the corner of his eye.

He'd have liked everyone to be there, for no other reason than to protect him if Lydia decided he was out of his mind.

Kneeling down in front of her, he pulled a single diamond solitaire from his pocket and held it up to her. "I don't want to wait one more moment to ask you to marry me. I want you to be my wife. I want to have more children with you. I love you. Nothing has ever stopped me from loving you and nothing ever will. Marry me, Lydia. Let's make up for lost time and create a new future."

He heard the gasps coming from the doorway, and he assumed that even more people had joined the others who had been there. He didn't turn around.

Lydia held out her shaking hand and Phillip took it, holding the ring at the tip of her finger.

"Well, is that a yes?" he asked looking up at her.

Lydia nodded, unable to make her words audible through her tears.

Phillip slipped the ring on her finger and stood, gathering her in his arms. "Forever, Lydia. I meant it when I was twenty-one, I mean it now."

CHAPTER 35

*T*he driver pulled the car into the cemetery, and a parade of other cars followed. Phillip held Lydia's hand as they sat silently in the back seat waiting for the driver to open the door.

"Are you doing okay?" he asked her, and Lydia nodded.

"It was hard enough fifteen years ago, but this time, I don't know, it finally seems real. She didn't have a funeral, and she should have. I was the only one who knew where she was."

"She's home now, where she should be. I understand now that she would have died no matter what, but she'll never be forgotten."

Lydia rested her head on his shoulder. In the past month, she'd spent more time apologizing for everything, and he'd reassured her that there was nothing to be sorry for. Circumstances from years before would not dictate their future.

Lydia could see Emma's tiny casket waiting for them and the sprays of flowers that surrounded her new resting place. Before the driver opened her door, she saw her entire family emerge from their cars. Every member of the Walker family and a group of officers in full uniform, walked toward their daughter.

The driver extended his hand to Lydia who stepped out of the car, followed by Phillip. Her mother, who had sat in the front seat, joined them, hooking her hand with Lydia's as Phillip slipped her arm around her. His mother and father joined them as they walked to the grave.

They sat next to the grave of their daughter as a minister gave his sermon. Their family surrounding them, and arrangements of flowers, sent from each of the families adorned their daughter's casket. She was loved. They all were loved.

Emma Grace was home.

LYDIA'S HOUSE WAS LEASED, after Russell had done a quick remodel on it. She'd taken possession of townhouse and that, too, had been leased.

The *Bridal Mecca* was being erected slowly, with its new second story, which would have a communal workspace, and Todd would manage the area. They already had leases on the private offices.

Lydia Morgan stood in the bridal suite at *The Garden Room* on the warm Saturday in August and looked at herself in the mirror. Pearl moved in behind her and fitted the veil on her head and attached it.

For the first time in her life, she was front and center when it came to bridal preparations. Phillip hadn't wanted to waste any more time not being man and wife. He'd done everything he could to assure Lydia had a unique, and beautiful wedding, as quickly as possible.

"You're exquisite," Pearl said as she looked at Lydia in the mirror. Chelsea fixed the train, and Missy rested her hands on her stomach as she nodded her approval.

Audrey had done her hair earlier that morning, and Nichole had followed up with her makeup. Bethany had designed the flowers, and Gia had given her an embroidered handkerchief she'd brought back from her hometown of Lucca, Italy. Jessie stood to the side of the room and photographed all of them together. Ella watched the festivities with a glass of champagne as Susan filled more glasses with so they could all celebrate.

These were her sisters, Lydia thought as she acknowledged them all as she looked in the mirror. She'd stood outside the Walker family her entire life looking in, and now she was as much a part of the family as many of these women.

Her mother walked into the room, and Susan handed her a glass.

"They are ready for you," she said. "Phillip looks handsome, and I can honestly say, I've never seen a more nervous groom. Your brother is doing his best to keep him calm with all the Walker men surrounding him."

Lydia laughed, because she knew if she spoke, she'd start to cry.

She looked in the mirror again, and touched her fingers to a locket that Phillip had given to her as a wedding gift. Inside, on one side there was a picture of her and him years ago when they'd first fell in love. On the other side was a picture of Emma Grace, one of the only pictures Lydia ever had of her.

The women all gathered together in a circle and took a glass of champagne from the tray that Susan held.

Pearl held her glass high, looking beautiful in her satin rose bridesmaid's dress.

"To Lydia, whose dreams of owning the entire town have helped each and every one of us. To the only woman I know who could endure and thrive. And to the last of us," she looked at Jessie who smiled, "well, almost the last of us to walk down the aisle. I still can't believe you're going to marry Phillip Smythe, but I couldn't be happier."

The women collectively lifted their glasses in a toast, and then surrounded Lydia in a group embrace.

CHAPTER 36

*P*hillip adjusted his tie for the third time before his father stepped in and straightened it for him. He gave him a supportive pat on the back and stepped away so Phillip could continue to fuss over the tuxedo, which felt awkward and formal.

Tyson appeared in the mirror behind him, looking equally uncomfortable in his tuxedo. "You look like you're going to pass out, man."

"I'm just wishing time would pass faster. I've waited so long for this moment, and I'm afraid she'll back out."

Tyson rested a hand on his shoulder. "She never would," he said with a chuckle.

Around the room sat the men who had been with Phillip through the past decade. His future brother-in-law would stand with him as witness to his marriage. Todd, Gerald, Ben, Eric, Kent, Gregory, Jake, Russell, and Dane moved into toward him each with a shot glass filled with whisky.

"To you, Phillip. Damn if I ever thought today would come to fruition," Tyson joked as he wrapped an arm around Phillip's shoulders. "You've been good to my sister, even when she didn't deserve it. I wish you a lifetime of happiness."

The men all held up their glasses and shot back the liquid.

As they all dispersed, Phillip stood in front of the mirror again, pulling his new pocket watch from his pocket—a gift from Lydia. Inside was the only photo ever taken of her and their baby girl. He would cherish the gift for the rest of his life.

THE GARDEN ROOM was filled with friends and family who had all gathered to celebrate Phillip's marriage to the woman he'd always loved. He had to assume there were some guests there just to see if the wedding actually played out. How could he blame them?

The front half of the room was filled with the Walker family, from both sides. Oh, hadn't they all had their trials and triumphs? He'd been there for all of it, good and bad. Beyond them were those who served the community with him. He was blessed beyond belief.

And then he saw her.

On her mother's arm, Lydia, the most beautiful woman he'd ever seen in his life, walked toward him in a simple white satin gown that fitted to her small frame and gave her the elegance of a princess.

He couldn't help when tears escaped his eyes and rolled down his cheeks.

The closer they came to him, he knew that the day had been made just for the two of them to start over. Today they would marry in front of their family and friends. Tomorrow they would start a new life, which they had already decided would include at least four more children.

Phillip realized he hadn't heard a word the minister had said, all he knew was that Lydia moved to him and took his hand. He simply couldn't help himself, he moved both of his hands to her face and kissed her.

She laughed sweetly as she eased back. "It's not time for that."

"It's always time for that."

As she took his hands that lingered on her cheeks, she noticed something on his wrist. Gently, she pushed back the cuff of his jacket.

"You got a new tattoo," she whispered and he smiled down at her as she admired the design that matched hers.

"I'll keep her with me for eternity too, Lydia."

Lydia let out a breath and gazed up into his eyes. "Here we are. At last. You and me."

"At last," he repeated. "Forever."

EPILOGUE

*P*hillip had been called to the hospital in the middle of a traffic stop. Usually he wasn't the one pulling over drivers, but when the woman in the blue Civic ran the red light right in front of him, he had no choice.

It had been Pearl who had called, and immediate panic had nearly paralyzed his heart and labored his breathing.

He'd rushed through the doors of the hospital to find Sunshine by the elevators waiting for him. "They're on the fourth floor." She pressed the buttons and sent him on his way.

When the doors opened, Pearl met him and took his hand. "C'mon."

"Is she okay? Tell me she's fine."

"You need to get in there."

"Pearl," he said again, stopping before they went through the double doors. "Is she okay? I mean it. Don't lie to me."

"She's fine, but her water broke and you need to hurry."

Phillip gripped the pocket watch in his pocket and held it tightly in his hand. "It's early. This is too early." He opened the watch and looked down at the picture of Lydia and their daughter.

"With this kind of pregnancy, this is normal."

Pearl took his hand again and pulled him through the doors and to the room where they were prepping Lydia.

"God, I thought you were going to miss this," she said as a contraction ripped through her.

"Never. Never ever." He moved to her and took her hand. "You're going to do a great job."

"Get in my purse. I have picture of Emma and I want to have her with us."

Phillip did as she'd asked as the doctor hurried into the room.

"Lydia, we have to take you in for a C-section."

She raised on her elbow and narrowed her eyes on the doctor. "That's not what we planned. No."

"Lydia," he said resting a hand on her belly. "Baby A has moved and is now breech. The only way we can get to it is to C-section and then we'll take baby B at the same time. They're both healthy and safe. You will be too."

Phillip pressed a kiss to her forehead. "She's watching over you, Lydia. You can do this."

AN HOUR after they had rushed Lydia into surgery, Phillip walked into the waiting room where each and every one of the Walkers had filled the room, along with Lydia's mother, and his parents.

Pearl moved to him, her own daughter on her hip. "Well? She did great, right?"

Phillip smiled wide. "She was fantastic. Walker was born first. He was five pounds, eight ounces."

"Isn't that small?" Everett Walker asked.

"Not for a twin." Phillip wiped his hand over the back of his neck. "Morgan weighed in at six pounds. She's going to forever keep her big brother in check," he humored as he wiped joyful tears from his eyes.

Pearl pulled him to her. "I'm so happy for you both. I can't wait to meet them."

LYDIA LAY IN HER BED, both of her babies rested against her bare breasts. Phillip had gone to announce their birth.

She kissed each baby on top of their heads.

"Did your sister pick you special just for us? When I look in your eyes, I know that she did. Just so you know, I'm so grateful for both of you. I love your daddy so much."

"And their daddy loves you," Phillip's voice came from the doorway.

"I think Walker looks just like you," she said as he reached for the little boy and held him to his chest.

"I just can't imagine who these two precious babies will become. They're just perfect."

"They are." Lydia reached for his hand. "I've never been so happy in my life," she said, and a single tear rolled down her cheek.

"Neither have I. At last, I have you all to myself," Phillip said, and Lydia laughed.

"At last we all have one another."

MEET THE AUTHOR

Bestselling Author Bernadette Marie is known for building families readers want to be part of. Her series The Keller Family has graced bestseller charts since its release in 2011. Since then she has authored and published over thirty-five books. The married mother of five sons promises romances with a Happily Ever After always…and says she can write it because she lives it.

Obsessed with the art of writing and the business of publishing, chronic entrepreneur Bernadette Marie established her own publishing house, 5 Prince Publishing, in 2011 to bring her own work to market as well as offer an opportunity for fresh voices in fiction to find a home as well.

When not immersed in the writing/publishing world, Bernadette Marie and her husband are shuffling their five hockey playing boys around town to practices and games as well as running their family business. She is a lover of a good stout craft beer and might have an unhealthy addiction to chocolate.

Masterpiece *Bernadette Marie*
A Tropical Christmas *Bernadette Marie*
Corporate Christmas *Bernadette Marie*
Faith Through Falling Snow *Sandy Sinnett*
After School Adventure: Beyond the Briar Patch *Antony Soehner*
Walker Defense *Bernadette Marie*
Clash of the Cheerleaders *April Marcom*
Stevie-Girl and the Phantom of Forever *Ann Swann*
Assemble the Party *Antony Soehner*
The Last Goodbye *Bernadette Marie*
The Gingerbread Curse *April Marcom*
Stevie-Girl and the Phantom of Crybaby Bridge *Ann Swann*
The MacBrides: Hannah & Ash *J.L. Petersen*
Leather and Lies *Celeste Straub*
Beginnings *Bernadette Marie*
Love and Loopholes *Railyn Stone*
Unite The Party *Antony Soehner*
Star Seer *April Marcom*
Totally Devoted *E.M. Bannock*
Bases Loaded *Jena James*

Visit our website at
www.5princebooks.com
For even more titles from amazing authors.

Made in the USA
Coppell, TX
08 July 2022

79723877R00121